Nietzsche's kisses

Nietzsche's kisses

lance olsen

FC2
NORMAL/TALLAHASSEE

Published by FC2 with support provided by Florida State University
and the Publications Unit of the Department of English at Illinois State
University

Address all inquiries to: Fiction Collective Two, Florida State University,
c/o English Department, Tallahassee, FL 32306-1580

ISBN-10: Paper, 1-57366-127-9
ISBN-13: Paper, 978-1-57366-127-0

Library of Congress Cataloging-in-Publication Data
Olsen, Lance, 1956-
  Nietzsche's kisses / Lance Olsen. — 1st ed.
    p. cm.
  ISBN 1-57366-127-9 (pbk.)
  1. Nietzsche, Friedrich Wilhelm, 1844-1900—Death and burial
—Fiction. 2. Philosophers—Germany—Death—Fiction.   I. Title.
PS3565.L777N54 2006
813'.54--dc22

                                        2005036751

Cover Design: Lou Robinson
Book Design: Tara Reeser

Produced and printed in the United States of America
Printed on recycled paper with soy ink

Also by Lance Olsen

NOVELS
Live from Earth
Tonguing the Zeitgeist
Burnt
Time Famine
Freaknest
Girl Imagined by Chance
10:01

SHORT STORIES
My Dates with Franz
Scherzi, I Believe
Sewing Shut My Eyes
Hideous Beauties

NONFICTION
Ellipse of Uncertainty
Circus of the Mind in Motion
William Gibson
Lolita: A Janus Text
Rebel Yell: A Short Guide to Writing Fiction

Acknowledgments

Excerpts from what follows first appeared in slightly different versions in *Black Ice*, *English Studies Forum*, *Fantastic Metropolis*, *Gargoyle*, *Indiana Review*, *Metastatic Whatnot*, *Northwest Edge: Fictions of Mass Destruction*, and *Potion*. In addition to Nietzsche's own work, essential to this novel's composition were R. J. Hollingdale's *Nietzsche: The Man and His Philosophy*, Christopher Middleton's edition of *Selected Letters of Friedrich Nietzsche*, and Rüdiger Safranski's *Nietzsche: A Philosophical Biography*. Andi Olsen and R.M. Berry offered many important and extraordinarily helpful suggestions for revision. The NEA provided support and time to see this book to fruition. To all, my deepest thanks.

for Andi, where the smiling begins

One must pay dearly for immortality: one
must die several times while still alive.
—Nietzsche, *Ecce Homo*

Only the day after tomorrow belongs to
me. Some are born posthumously.
—Nietzsche, *The Antichrist*

first part:
on the despisers of the body

5 p.m.

Every sentence is a kiss.

Yes, that's it: I searched and searched for them through the tenement inside my head and presto—they suddenly rejoin the conversation.

All the voices of history.

All the voices of history speaking to me.

Prince Bismarck being a good student—never a prodigy, mind you, never a sensation, but a solid worker nonetheless.

Every sentence is a kiss and every paragraph an embrace.

The skin sensing it.

Unless, of course, history's chatter happens to be mistaken.

There's always that possibility.

There's always that possibility among others.

In any case, this flawless morning will unfold into a flawless day. I am sure of it. If it is morning, that is, and not, say, twilight. Twilight being another possibility for what it is.

Right, here I go: the extravagance.

Let us call it the opening of the eyes.

Give it a second.

Give it a second.

More light.

It seems I can no longer feel my fingers.

I can smell time, but I can no longer feel my fingers and I can no longer feel my feet. Insignificant concerns on a day rich with such promise as this, yet it appears as if…what? It appears as if my limbs simply evanesce into air as they extend away from me.

Only yesterday the prince was capering, and now, lying beneath these hot sheets on this flawless morning, sweating, sweating and thinking, sweating and endeavoring to think, he is about to undertake the opening of his eyes.

In order to have a look around me.

There occurs movement involving the lower portion of my face, mollusk plumped on the floor of my mouth.

When my bowels last roused themselves in an attempt to stage a modest display is anyone's guess.

It could, for all I know, come to think of it, still be the middle of the night.

There is nothing to prevent it.

Unless, obviously, my eyes are already open.

There is always that.

Unless my eyes are already open and have been for let us say hours or days, in which case I have finally gone blind.

Such an event would arrive as no real surprise.

Listen closely: you can hear my clothing.

My hospital gown breathing.

I should perhaps take this opportunity to point out I would much rather be a Basel professor than God and yet, alas, one is who one is—until one isn't who one is, naturally, at which heart thump one is someone else.

The general impression I want to say being that of drifting in a fog on Lake Lucerne.

On holiday once, on holiday in Tribschen, I launched from Wagner's dock at the edge of the yellow splash of wildflowers: the city's spires, the fountains, the church bells reaching me from the far side of the water, the spring sun rushing over my shoulders.

I rowed east toward the rocky horizon, bagful of chocolates on the seat beside me, until my arms ached, then pulled in the oars and lay back in the belly of my boat to lose myself in sugar and reflection.

I must have dozed because when I opened my eyes again everything was slate cloud, and, sitting up, I discovered the universe had disappeared.

I could barely even make out the lakewater lapping my craft's side.

I raised my oars and began to row. Pushing through the gray veils, I had the intimation it would take me all night to reach land. I therefore altered my course, only to find myself worrying I had altered it for the worse, that prior to this alteration I had been rowing in more or less the correct direction.

Imagine: the abrupt moment of contact with shore never coming.

It felt as if I would row on and on through emptiness forever.

I want to say now, here, lying beneath these hot sheets, sweating, sweating and endeavoring to think, it is precisely the same sensation, only in time.

I can no longer seem to remember whether I'm remembering or believing I'm remembering when I'm not remembering at all.

I want to say I holidayed in Tribschen.

I want to say I did not.

Every day people tell me the most remarkable things about my life.

They recount, by way of illustration, the quiet evenings I shared with this friend or that.

Did I by any chance enjoy myself? I ask.

It matters to me, you see.

And so what I shall do next is this: I shall undertake the opening of my eyes…like this…yes…like this…there they go…the great extravagance…and there is a dark shape fluttering back and forth in front of me, a huge black insect against the bright white window.

A woman, I am fairly sure.

A diminutive woman moving.

She steps out of the glare, draws alongside my bed, and the damp sheets are off me, her hands between my legs.

She works diligently, although my sense of touch isn't what it used to be.

Massaging, conceivably, or, conceivably, scrubbing.

Yes, that's it: she hums to herself, something sodden and German by Schubert, looking familiar, looking very familiar, her long gray hair piled into a frizzy bun, purple cobwebs spun across her raw cheeks, scrubbing.

Are you perhaps my mother? I ask, breaking the silence, mouth all slurry.

She doesn't look up.

Then, *voilà*, this crookshelled apparition withdraws a bedpan from what appears to be a sizeable hole in the mattress between my legs and divines its liquid contents before releasing a small winged smile into the humidity.

It's Alwine, Fritz, she says, smiling. Do you know me?

Of course I know you, I respond, slow and slurry, studying her features. You've been with us... You've been with the family... since I was Vittorio.

Vittorio?

Vittorio Emanuele. Yes, obviously.

She lowers the bedpan.

They're back, then? she asks.

A little.

And what did they tell you?

Oh...well. You know. This and that.

She consults the harsh window, the harsh door.

I know, I say. I'm sorry.

Listen to me, she says, turning back. You're Fritz this afternoon, Fritz. You were Fritz yesterday afternoon. And tomorrow afternoon? Tomorrow afternoon you will be Fritz again. Are you hungry? Your sister is coming by. She's bringing visitors. You need to eat. A bowl of cabbage soup? A bowl of cabbage soup and slice of bread? I've baked some fresh.

While contemplating the question, it occurs to me there is a woman standing in the room.

I beg your pardon, I say, but your name is...

Alwine, Fritz. Alwine.

Do you want to know a secret, Alwine-Fritz-Alwine?

If you don't eat, do you know what your sister will do?

I look up at the ceiling.

She will accuse Alwine of not feeding her Fritz. Do you want to get Alwine into trouble?

I look up at the ceiling, then lower my gaze to this person who, for some reason, strikes me as someone you can trust.

I whisper to her:

Every sentence is a kiss.

What?

Every sentence is a kiss, I repeat, louder, *and every paragraph an embrace.*

She stands there watching the show called Friedrich, then raises the bedpan like a Sunday roast on a serving tray, turns, and, careful not to spill a drop of me, makes her way toward the door.

Fritz, she says over her shoulder. Fritz. What are we going to do with you?

A good question.

The door opens. The universe pauses. The door clicks shut.

Everywhere wind surging into cognition.

Everywhere noise without end.

tail

And next you are overboard thrashing to stay afloat. You were standing in your rowboat balancing charily in an attempt to get your bearings your oar a cane then your legs kicked out from under you and now your rowboat is dissolving into the fog and evening contaminating the dampness and your oar must have hit you because there is lightning at the bridge of your nose. Frost is gathering on the tissues of your heart and there is lightning at the bridge of your nose and you stretch your left shoe down to poke for bottom and there is nothing below you nothing in any direction and the idea sends you beneath the waves in a scattered flux of panic and up again like a human balloon buoying choking snot and blood streaming through your mustache. You reach down to untie your shoes kick off their weight but realize with alarm you can't feel your hands your feet are bars of peacockblue pain dangling. What might be your fingers graze against what might be your laces only your joints don't bend there is live water in your mouth and up your runny nose and you are thinking *what doesn't kill me makes me stranger*. You swam as a child at the Pforta school and there were many better students than you and you read until your vision bleared in the evening trying to make up for your shortfalls and you swam and skated with the other boys and loved how swimming made you into a penguin bulleting across the pond. They woke you at four o'clock every morning save Sunday and you had to be ready for class by six and then you had a break at four then dinner then more classes and bedtime was nine and if you were lucky you had perhaps an hour to yourself all day. When you were twelve or thirteen your head caught fire for the first time and the pondwater made the flames more intense and you are losing sensation your muscles hardening everything very quick. You would push for the boat if you knew which way to push but the oar knocked off your glasses and the fog is consolidating and you slide beneath the waves a second time. It surprises you so much you instinctively shoot up breach choking thrashing bleeding snotting thinking *happiness is a complicated phenomenon* because there is nowhere to go nothing to do except what you are doing. There is nowhere to go nothing to do and it occurs to you you have probably been here before will probably be here again because in infinity there is just so much matter so many worlds then they begin repeating themselves and in all likelihood you have visited this one before and in some variations you have drowned and in some you have survived and in some you never rented the rowboat in the first place but sat under a shade tree on a bench on the dock at Tribschen and ate your bag of chocolates stuffed with marzipan paste and this is why Darwin is a thinking monkey. Evolution takes us nowhere because progress is a ring we have had tails we have tails we will have tails once more and all we can do is swallow them. If you had to undergo the present formulation three thousand times four thousand ten would you have the courage and what sort of courage would this be an example of if you only had to go under once and in the midst of that thought you become aware of your rowboat gliding unhurriedly out of a fog bank into the open and you squint unable to believe your good fortune because the thing is no more than two meters away from you it hasn't gone anywhere all you have to do is swim reach out hoist yourself in and this is how the present formulation of the story will write itself these are the contours it will take except. Except. Except this isn't how the present formulation will write itself because when you try to lift your arms to swim they don't lift and when you try to will your-self forward you slip beneath the waves struck by how shockingly cold the first inhalation is a mallet against your lungs you feel as if you are floating above yourself your body convulsing then you are smiling yes as you begin floating down trying to smile trying to smile and of course failing.

music without a future

My head is filled with Friedrich, Friedrich announces to no one, stepping out of his mother's house at number 18 Weingarten and pausing at the threshold.

She told him to wait for her to accompany him to the market.

It is Naumburg. It is 1890. Bismarck is gone, Zanzibar is going, and the Kaiser's new direction is no direction at all. Still, it is May and it will be a flawless day. There is no doubt about it.

Friedrich narrates these facts and the morning's fineness aloud for his own benefit. It helps him arrange the convolution of things.

How, above the cream and mustard houses, above their terra-cotta fishscale roofs, the sky's early whiteblue is tinged with an ambient gold scintillation. How the chill promises cool sunshine the second he moves from the shadows and how everything in the lives of these people undertaking their morning ceremonies in the street before him feels as if it has been revived.

Friedrich inhales deeply.

Green air. Horse hide. The last coal fires of the season.

This is what time smells like.

Across the narrow lane, a young woman with dark pulled-back hair reaches through her second-story window to tend a box of newly planted geraniums on the sill and she reminds Friedrich of someone he once knew and he knows everything will come easily today.

Everything will succeed.

What uncomplicated astonishment to stand here at the brink of a day like this.

He pronounces the words under his breath, telling, the most important thing surely being to get the present formulation right.

The wonderful cleanliness of his task nearly overwhelms him.

His head is filled with Friedrich, overfilled, and the point of living is the discovery of how to express that fullness in surprising ways. He loves his own company because he has never met better. Obviously, he would on no account admit such a notion to anyone else (except, needless to say, in his writing, which no one reads) for fear of hurting their feelings, but the truth is that other people make him intensely lonely. They make him awkward in the face of their intellectual awkwardness. Their minds don't dance. They lumber. Their public opinions are their private laziness.

No: he prefers talking to his equal.

He cherishes the thrill of strolling along the streets of a complex town or, better, across the grassy grayblue countryside, silhouettes of trees hazing hilltops, arguing with himself, contradicting himself, trying to catch himself out and laughing at the insights his mind gives rise to without warning.

What will he think next?

He can hardly wait to find out.

Once, he lost his way hiking in the mountains surrounding Sils-Maria because he was so deeply engaged in an elegant conversation with himself he forgot to pay attention to the landmarks. His sister, visiting at the time, called the local authorities when he didn't return home by nightfall. The police came around promptly and asked her for a description of the man for whom they were to mount a search.

If he's conscious, Lisbeth had told them, he's talking.

What a splendid line for such a splendid day.

He reaches into the inside breast pocket of his charcoal suit and withdraws the small notebook and stubby pencil he always carries with him.

Hesitates.

Looks up.

Adjusts his glasses with his thumb.

He is wearing his most powerful pair, the pair with the distorting lenses, and still existence arrives through a steam bath.

The ambient gold scintillation suffusing the whiteblue sky above the houses, above their terra-cotta fishscale roofs, is waxing into an ambient silver scintillation, every minute becoming something else.

This past autumn, he writes in a tight, vertical, almost Arabic scrawl, *I was blinded as little as possible when I twice witnessed my own funeral.*

He contemplates the line and, satisfied, closes the notebook and slips it back into place, with the pencil.

Sometimes Friedrich is embarrassed by how happy Friedrich

can be, Friedrich announces to no one, and, forgetting exactly why he is waiting here when such a glorious morning beckons, he gently clicks the heavy front door shut behind him, glances at the medieval wall his mother's house looks out upon, confirms the tilt of his charcoal topper, and launches into the shimmering possibility called the future.

Stepping into the lane, his hands rise up around his head like delicate white birds that will help explain to him what it is he is thinking now, what he is thinking now, what now.

It is the kind of happiness, the kind of uncomplicated astonishment, he felt almost exactly eight years ago one afternoon in Rome.

It was late April. It was 1882. Friedrich was visiting Malwida von Meysenbug, the feisty, squat, universal aunt to nomadic German-speaking freethinkers everywhere. He strolled into her sitting room after a long constitutional through the filthy city and happened upon a beautiful young woman with dark pulled-back hair reading one of his books on the sofa.

Friedrich could make out the cover from where he fetched up: *Human, All Too Human.*

He had sketched and written a good part of it while wintering at Malwida's villa on the coast near Sorrento several years before. He occupied a big high room there with a terrace outside and nothing to distract him from his work aside from the rampant gardens, the luxurious afternoon teas with the other guests, and a nearly overpowering view across the open sea to Naples and Vesuvius, a sloped molar hanging in the distance.

Upon its publication, he had given a copy to Malwida by way of thanks. Apparently, it had followed her north. Friedrich always experienced a jolt seeing someone reading something he had written. His books existed for him deep inside his organs. A swish of trespass accompanied the flush of enchantment he felt whenever someone held a piece of him in her hands. She could just as well have been holding his lungs. Even so, his spirit lifted and the woman on the sofa looked up and her eyes glinted in recognition.

She inserted a silk tassel (just past his book's center), closed the covers and, without rising, said in a diaphanous Russian accent:

Herr Nietzsche. It is a great pleasure to make your and your will to power's acquaintance.

He was thirty-eight and she was twenty-one and yet language left him, leaving him disarmed and scratching the side of his face.

He wasn't good at matters of action.

Thinking on his feet terrified him.

Is it true, then, she continued, that even our deeds and sentiments not obviously connected with a desire for control are nonetheless prompted by it? I had never contemplated Christ's tolerance and meekness in quite those terms. I am certain clergy the world over would stand enlightened.

Friedrich took pleasure in the way she had made a conscious decision not to rise from the sofa upon his entrance. He took pleasure in her wasp-waisted black dress with the exquisite white lace extending from its wrists and high collar. And, most of all, he took pleasure in the way her dark pulled-back hair and pale skin and sharp intelligence spread through the room like a crackling charge of electricity.

Scratching, enjoying, Friedrich became aware of himself being aware again.

He couldn't help it. His mind was a mouse in a maze. Language resettled his head syllable by syllable. He let his hand fall to his side and tried to straighten his back into something like poise.

That, I suspect, is why I wrote the thing in the first place, he replied.

As he did so, fairly pleased with his response, a much older woman, who reminded him of nothing so much as a blackboard eraser topped with a feathered hat, appeared in the doorway leading from the hall and embarked on calibrating this neighborhood's significance and the significance of the two people inhabiting it.

She narrowed her eyes in a manner that gave Friedrich the inkling she found everything except perhaps the small jade statue of Shiva on the hectic fireplace mantel lacking.

Ah, said the young woman on the sofa, half-turning and presenting her palm in the older woman's general direction without actually meeting her eyes...my mother, Frau Salomé.

Her voice sounded a little fatigued, as if she had pronounced those words in the recent past more times than she might have strictly relished.

...And, said the eraser with no accent whatsoever, my daughter, whom I suspect hasn't quite had the opportunity to break away from sharing her opinions long enough to introduce herself. Fräulein Salomé. Louise.

I... Friedrich began, but the eraser wasn't done.

...Although everyone, it seems, despite the fact I am honestly at a loss to understand why, takes the liberty of calling her Lou. Herr Professor Nietzsche, it is a very great honor meeting you. Malwida has spoken libraries of praise about you. Louise, please come along. We are late for our meeting with some ruins. Good lord, I have never in my life seen more fallen rocks than on our current journey. This, I take it, is what the Italians refer to as "culture"? Fine, then. Fine. Bring on the quarries...

It was childish, Friedrich announces, hands fluttering up by his ears.

It was childish and it was naïve and it lacked edge and yet the reality remains he loved Lou instantly and loved her completely.

He rounds a corner onto a cobblestone lane lined with colorful shops. Ahead, St. Wenzel's gothic dunce cap lifts into view. Pedestrians veer out of his path. They pretend they don't hear him, can't see him, but he can tell in his presence they shy closer to the shop fronts.

Friedrich is pleased.

It is time people began noticing him.

For years, the surprise has been how few have. It is a continual blow to his well-being how virtually no one in Germany, let alone the rest of Europe, is thinking about him at any given moment on any given day. How could such a thing have come to pass?

Granted: a handful of friends used to read his books with passion and admiration. They used to write to tell him so. They used to argue through the post and in the newspapers and the arguments were delicious. But then, one by one, they commenced falling away. Their letters became insignificant, respectable, benevolent, remote—less than shopping lists of tedious activities and superficial emotions embodied in thoughtless prose—and then they ceased altogether. For more than a decade now, he has brought out on average one book a year, recently at his own expense. Only sixty or seventy copies of each of the first three parts of *Zarathustra* sold. He could only afford to print forty copies of the fourth. He ended up giving away seven simply to make sure someone would look at it, and even then there was no evidence anyone did.

Presently there is almost no one out there unless it is some idiot reviewer readying to launch some idiot assault, or some one-time friend badmouthing his brain to various Wagnerites behind his back.

Or, worse, no reviewer and no one-time friend and no assault at all, just stillness and calm in the wake of a new work's appearance…and there is nothing worse than stillness and calm in the wake of a new work's appearance.

He is positive, or very nearly so, he remembers Lisbeth, or perhaps it was Overbeck or Burckhardt—someone close to him, at any rate, yes, he is confident of that—writing to inform him that a critic delivered a series of lectures outlining his philosophy somewhere up north two or three years ago.

Give it a second.

Give it a second.

Georg Brandes, yes: that Great Dane with the large intellect at the University of Copenhagen.

Which is to say…what?

The superb sky leaves no question about it at all.

When he walks down the street, pedestrians pay attention. When he enters one of these shops, every face changes. Women gaze after him as he tests vegetables for firmness and in the market he is sure the sexy young things hold back the sweetest grapes for him.

On occasion, they have been known to lower the price of fish in his honor.

That evening, in the antique city, he showed up at Malwida's dinner table fifteen minutes early in his best suit.

The very suit, in point of fact, he is wearing this morning: charcoal brown with matching vest, gold watch fob, lilac shirt, and wide daffodil-yellow tie one can hear buzzing like a furry bee on a summer window pane if one listens closely enough.

Friedrich left his charcoal topper behind in his room, where he spent the better part of an hour trimming and combing his mustache, the fever vision cycling behind his brow that something (cheesy soups and clotty sauces were the most alarming) would become netted in it while he dined. The rest of the company would thereby be forced to observe him go about his gastronomical business, things hanging off him, for hours on end. The image was insufferable.

He stood patiently behind his chair, waiting in the empty dining room, worrying, raising his fingers to confirm the current state of his mustache, lowering them, raising them again just to make absolutely sure he hadn't by any chance missed anything, that the grain of his whiskers remained in perfect vertical alignment.

Friedrich was so early because he couldn't abide lateness.

The act of being late implied one of two untenable philosophical positions: either the belief in an utter lack of free will, or the calculated domination by one human being over another for no particular reason. *My time is more important than yours*, the tardy person always proclaims by his or her act. *You will wait for me.*

Earliness was consequently a mark of respect, a kind of temporal equality, and so Friedrich waited behind his chair, thinking nothing of it, unwearied and erect as a guard standing at attention before a palace gate.

Malwida and her maid were first to bustle in. The former was a fuss of hugs and air kisses, the latter all grimness and solicitude. A ghastly old Polish couple followed. They suggested to Friedrich well-dressed armadillos walking on their hind legs, and they defiled sad mad Hölderlin by reciting his verse out loud to each other in overly theatrical voices, then chortling knowingly in an attempt to impress those around them with their cultivation. Initially Friedrich was certain they were French. They were nothing if not French. Then he thought they must be Sicilian. Sicilian or perhaps Spanish.

But, no: they were Polish.

How horribly odd.

Last, Lou and her mother materialized accompanied, surprisingly, by Friedrich's good friend, Paul Rée, with whom Friedrich had just passed late February and early March in Genoa. Rée was large-nosed, small-mouthed, black-suited, and bowtied. Friedrich considered him a pioneer in the psychological approach to the problems of philosophy. Five years Friedrich's junior, Rée maintained religion was nothing save an assortment of uninteresting fairy tales and ghost stories, morality a succession of bad habits. He wrote his *Origin of the Moral Sensations* at Sorrento the same time Friedrich was there composing *Human, All Too Human*, and it was Rée's courageous manuscript and their long agreeable conversations over tea on that terrace that made Friedrich's book possible.

Settling into his seat amid the fluffing of napkins and clearing of throats, Rée told how he had let inertia carry him south from one pretty Italian town to the next. He found himself here a week ago, when he had had the good fortune to meet the Salomés, with whom he was presently exploring various local sites in order to pass the onset of spring. This story led over appetizers into one by Lou's mother encompassing a detailed catalogue of the rubble they had visited so far. Stone, stone, stone, she said, temple, basilica, duomo. She was first to concede that she was no great expert on the topic, and yet she simply could not help expressing honest puzzlement before a civilization unable to feel at least the shadow of humility for proving on an almost hourly basis that its most fecund days, intellectually, politically, and artistically speaking, were nearly two millennia behind it. Could anyone by any chance help her?

Anyone could not, it turned out: a caesura rolled across the table, disrupted by the clinking of spoons against china and the relentless Polish couple, who had evidently forgotten they were dining with others.

Lou stared at the onion soup before her, tendons in her jaw flexing.

Friedrich looked up from his own bowl, whose contents he had been guiding into his mouth with profound care, and glimpsed his chance. He fortified himself, lifted his starched napkin, dabbed at his mustache, and asked her what had brought her mother and her down to Rome. Lou's eyes grazed off Friedrich's and rested on a far corner of the room as she gathered her thoughts. The maid removed the soup bowls and served plates eventful with thin slices of rare roast beef, potatoes au gratin, and string beans. Lou opened her mouth to speak, and Frau Salomé began answering for her.

She launched into an account of how Lou had been born in St. Petersburg, the daughter of a general of Huguenot extraction, and how, much to her parents' enormous displeasure, two years ago announced in no uncertain terms she was committed to leading a self-directed life.

Frau Salomé pronounced the adjective and noun in quotation marks.

Barely nineteen, Lou planned to leave Russia to attend university in Zürich. Frau Salomé insisted on accompanying her. Late last year, Lou fell ill with a malady of the lungs. A friend gave her a letter of introduction to Malwida, to whose house in Rome she had traveled to recuperate.

She arrived in January.

Three months later, Rée showed up.

At present, everything was this bath, that catacombs, and the other arch, each in various stages of disrepair.

Friedrich did his best to concentrate on what Frau Salomé was saying, only his attention kept wandering back to Lou. The glummer she seemed, picking bleakly through the food on her plate, the more he loved her. He wanted to rise and walk around the table and embrace her. He wanted to lead her out of this cramped house in this cramped city and take her north, into Switzerland, where they could see in spring together among the lakes and mountains.

Instead, he sat politely and focused on successfully piloting potatoes beneath his mustache, bided his time, and, later, once everyone had retired for the night, composed a brief note which he slipped beneath Lou's door.

From which stars, it said, *have we been brought together?*

He paced his room until he became concerned he might be keeping the rest of the house awake, then took a seat at his writing table before the window and watched lights gutter off down the street one by one as the red misty dawn collected.

At breakfast over hard-boiled eggs, ham, toast, and English marmalade, Friedrich took Lou's lack of response as an auspicious sign: despite all this talk of independence, all her palpable intelligence, she was clearly still in good part ingenuous and shy.

She feigned disinterest in him and, when she thought he was looking elsewhere, stole several glances in his direction.

Six years earlier, Friedrich had met and fallen in love with another shy independent woman named Mathilde at the house of a conductor-acquaintance of his, Hugo von Senger, in Geneva. It was April then, as well, and, like Lou, Mathilde was sharp, striking, and twenty-one. Five days after their meeting, they spent an enjoyable evening together discussing poetry and music. Unable to bring himself to raise the subject of marriage in person, Friedrich returned to his hotel and wrote her a concise, well-argued proposal, which he sent over by messenger. Mathilde turned him down by messenger first thing the next day and, not long after, married Senger.

The problem, Friedrich was convinced post factum, was the letter.

It was too emotionally distant, too dryly academic, by half.

Should a similar situation ever present itself, he would conduct himself in a forthright manner.

In a word, he would allow his spirit to speak openly.

That afternoon in Rome he waited until the Fräulein and Frau had retired to their respective rooms for naps, then cornered a startled Rée in the downstairs hallway as he exited the library. After some unavoidable small talk, Friedrich executed his strategy. He asked his friend if he would be so kind as to propose to Lou on his behalf at Rée's earliest possible convenience.

Would this evening conceivably be satisfactory? Friedrich asked.

His shoes sound like sandpaper in the square and so he pauses and steps out of them. There is too much din in the world already. He closes his eyes and feels the solar system corkscrewing around him.

When he opens them again, Friedrich finds himself standing in front of the ornate Rathaus. Across the square to his left is the statue of Saint Wenzel overseeing the fountain in his hat shaped like a shell. Behind him, on the eastern end, the town portal from 1680.

How, in the course of his life, did he arrive here?

At one time, there seemed to have been so many other places to go.

A handful of people drift across the square or sit at outdoor tables under red and white umbrellas reading newspapers, sipping morning coffee, nibbling pastries. Blinking, Friedrich tries to force them into focus, and slowly becomes aware of a headache glowing somewhere behind his eyes. It looks to him like a bluely burning coal.

He realizes his tie is too tight. He loosens it and pulls it through his collar. Friedrich tugs off his jacket, lets it fall to his feet and, blinking, loves, helplessly, the swaybacked horse harnessed to the old wooden cart near the statue, how the sunshine gleams off its mangy flanks. He loves the pigeons flurrying around the stooped woman in a black shawl, her arms outstretched like a scarecrow, bread crumbs in her upraised palms. He loves the fragrance of cinnamon tarts and cigarettes and horseshit in the air, the resonance of the church bells beginning to toll above these buildings, how the day's warmth speeds back and forth across this flesh.

He unbuttons his vest and removes it. He unbuttons his shirt and removes it. Reaching for his belt buckle, he appreciates Naumburg's tranquility. Its sense of understated purpose. How Germany comes to its conclusion in locations like this.

So much for him depends on the sky.

He removes his trousers and removes his socks and removes his undergarments and loves the two men in uniform making their way toward him from the café across the square, coffee cups still in their hands.

Behind them, he believes he can make out his mother waving.

Yes, Franziska: she is trotting to join him.

Where did she come from?

He looks forward to learning the answer.

Meanwhile, he smiles at her familiarly and stretches his bare arms out to his sides, mimicking the pigeon woman.

He shuts his eyes again and tilts his face to receive the incoming rays.

He concentrates deeply on distributing his love to every living thing that has forgotten him in this very special space.

6 p.m.

When the windstorm slackens, I open my eyes once more...yes... like this...and the light has changed.

White brightness now contains apricot traces.

It is either tomorrow again or simply more of today, but later.

I am, be that as it may, sweating.

Sweating profusely, lying beneath these hot sheets on this new day, this old day, or this continuation of the same day, sweating and thinking, sweating and endeavoring to think...unless, it almost goes without saying, I have wet myself.

My mother bought me a piano when I was six, incidentally, and there is no one to read to me.

Every evening I lie here waiting for permission to go to sleep.

Dampness extends down my back, buttocks, the verso of my thighs and calves.

The general impression, I want to say, is one of seasickness.

Batten down the witches. Secure the mainsoul. Plug your ears with vex and lash my nobody to the mist.

And so.

And so.

And so: I compose in my head to pass the timelessness.

Dearest Luminosity—

Please come collect me. I don't know where I am, but please come collect me. Tomorrow my son Petronius is visiting with his charming Ariadne and I shall greet them in my shirtsleeves. The prospect terrifies me. Meanwhile, doctors are in the process of crucifying me at great length. You should see their cravats.

We have no very serious professional duties, and this is what will save us.

Fondly,

Your Old Creature

Post Scriptum: Don't forget your string.

In the theater of my head, I watch Lou read what I have written. I watch us strolling through the poorly lit Roman streets after dark, talking about the will to power. There exists an incandescent moment when I contemplate reaching out and taking her hand in my hoof.

The moment passes.

When I open my eyes again the crookshelled woman is back, this time carrying a tray filled with threatening objects.

A bowl of soup.

A slice of bread.

Among others.

She is humming something that smells like a healthy German belch.

Erro, erras, errat.

It's just me, she says.

She sets down the tray on the bedside table, crosses the room, and returns with a wooden chair onto which she painstakingly lowers herself.

Great rump settling.

Where is my brother? I ask.

Joseph died when he was three, Fritz, and you…you were six. Five or six. A little boy. Do you remember?

She raises the bowl of soup and my favorite painted spoon.

My other brother… Him. The other. Peter.

Peter? Peter… Peter Gast? He was a nice young man for a Jew, wasn't he? You played piano together. Were you thinking of him just now?

She dips the spoon into cream green.

Will no one read to me?

First we eat, then maybe we read. You have guests visiting this evening. They believe you've thought many wonderful things.

The spoon advances.

Lisbeth will join them. Everyone wants to see what a great man looks like. Won't that be pleasant? But before we show them, we must eat and wash ourselves. Open your mouth. Tell me one of your great ideas.

The spoon ticks into the teeth I am baring at her.

I am going for a growl, the blond beast in the swaying bed.

The spoon withdraws.

She eyes me agreeably, calculating her options.

I gather my energy and blink back at her.

Repeatedly.

You want to get Alwine into trouble? she asks. Is this what you want? There will be a great ceremony. Do you want me to tell them the famous Friedrich Nietzsche won't eat his cabbage soup?

The spoon dips, rises, floats toward me.

A swollen second before it makes contact with my teeth again, she reaches forward matter-of-factly and pinches off my nostrils.

We have been here before.

We will be here again.

The galaxy comes to a standstill around us.

She waits. I wait. She waits. I wait.

She waits longer.

The spoon is in and out before I know it, cream green in my mouth, on my chin, speckled down my chest.

She strikes three more times before I am able to turn my face toward the wall.

Hope climbing out onto a ledge.

Hope leaning over.

teeth

And next you are wandering the aisles of a secondhand bookstore. You are twenty-one a student of philology and you have ducked out of the Leipzig cold this dismal November afternoon and there are obviously too many books on the planet. Those you should read but never will and those you believe you should read but discover halfway through you were wrong about and those you read against your better judgment because your friends have recommended them except your friends are no longer your friends and the politeness of the initial act has devolved into an attrition of days. The upsetting smell reminds you of dampness and the used-up-ness of empty libraries on winter evenings when you are the

only one inhabiting them reading by yourself at a large table while
the person at the reference desk does all he can to look occupied.
The other customers the broke students the grim Lutheran spinsters
and the store's owner with his reeky brown wool vest you can feel
every one of them watching you wander through the claustropho-
bic aisles trying to warm your hands debating whether you are here
to buy shoplift browse meet someone forming opinions about you
based on which aisle you choose which book you pick up how long
you take to examine and return it to its niche. You can sense them
trying to turn you into a book yourself but they can go to the devil
because you are an adult you have stopped going to Easter services
you will stand your ground. You leisurely reach up pick a volume
off the shelf in front of you at random begin thumbing through it
and without warning your life alters. Standing there among these
tomes these people you become somebody you weren't when you
woke up this morning. You just wanted to get out of the Leipzig
cold but you find yourself reading Schopenhauer's *The World as
Will and Idea* in a secondhand bookstore and his sentences aren't
angular like the sentences of other philosophers no but written
with gunpowder instead of ink. They aren't sentences at all *sentences*
being too soft a word for what they are they are *teeth*. Thumbing
turns into sampling a page here a page there turns into purchasing
the book turns into hurrying through the evening to your small flat
turns into two in the morning your head hurting your eyes hurting
but you can't stop reading. Here is the involuntary memoir of an
ex-medical student who slept with a loaded pistol under his pillow
arguing death is life's therapy arguing you should become alarmed
if nothing alarms you should become troubled if you are never
troubled loathe your skin cover yourself instead with intellect let
intellect use you because this is how you become a saint someone
who lives outside time outside space and need. Pass your passing
until deliverance delivers you from the willish jangle. This from

the man who remained embittered all his days disappointed un-
known until his last three years because the Hegelian sophists had
exhausted the thinking power of their generation with barbarous
and mysterious speech and then scared it away altogether from the
corpse of philosophy. This from the man who sixteen years after its
publication asked his publisher how many copies remained of his
book and was told very few and the publisher wasn't lying because
the numbers were low yet not because readers had bought it but
because the publisher had sold off the better part of the edition as
waste paper. Pass your passing until deliverance delivers you from
the willish jangle. This finally being the only thing Schopenhauer
could bring himself to say over and over hoping someone might
hear him talking to himself in Frankfurt and there you are listening
to him in this small flat up a dark flight of stairs dawn outside your
window you coming to appreciate something about the nature of
thought. You coming to appreciate that the errors of great men are
worthy of respect and admiration because they are more fruitful
than the truths of small men and this is why you will always adore
Schopenhauer and this is why reading him you will always experience the heart's frantic scramble.

misunderstanding of the dream

White mists drift through Friedrich's dreams by day and by night.

They wisp down in vaporous swells from the stark mountains around Sils-Maria and gust through the valleys, across Lake Zürich and Lake Constance, north into Germany, through Bavaria, up the Ilm river, into Weimar, across the crypt comforting the remains of Goethe and Schiller, through the front door of 18 Weingarten, up the flight of stairs, and deep into Friedrich's head.

They comprise the kind of light-flooded fog that conquers everything in a platinum glare and propels Friedrich from his bed in a single anxious push.

He is lying on his back, somewhere between waking and

sleeping, and then he is standing at the window, eyes so weak and fog so strong he can't see the other side of the street. The universe hovers in garish indistinctness. He can't recognize what town he is in. He can't remember what month he is in. He wants to say it is Tuesday, but he isn't sure why.

The only thing he knows with certainty is that his clammy hospital gown is clinging to his clammy buttocks in an unsightly way. He tugs it down and turns back to the room. None of the furniture is where it should be. The armchair, an unfamiliar maroon, rests in the middle of the floor, although he recalls it sitting next to the window, the wooden chair with floral designs on its backrest resides by his bed rather than by his writing desk, and his writing desk has vanished completely.

Scratching at his tailbone, Friedrich shuffles toward the door that will lead him out of this mess, steps through, and discovers himself inside a wardrobe. He plans for a while, exits, and finds himself staring down at his unkempt bed. He sets off and locates a door on the far side of the room, levers the latch, steps through, and finds himself standing on a very bright landing.

He can't remember ever having stood here before.

There is a small table on which perches a blue and white vase filled with blue and white flowers on a blue and white runner. A chocolate-brown crucifix hangs on the white wall above it. Next to the crucifix is a mirror. The stairwell is frightening.

Directly above, set into the low ceiling, is a pull-down ladder.

There are too many mirrors in the world. A matter of principle, Friedrich refuses to employ this one. The disconcerting truth about them, as with the act of copulation, is that they multiply the number of human beings.

He looks up at the ladder, at his pale hands birding out to tug the rope attached to the contraption. It lowers with Newtonian ease. Friedrich peers into the black lozenge above him and experiences the sensation of the universe having been turned upside down: he is peering into an inverted grave.

It occurs to him that this in actual fact may well be a Tuesday.

There is, in any case, nothing to prevent it.

Friedrich Nietzsche realizes he isn't particularly fond of Tuesdays.

The climb is not undemanding.

His stiff knees produce moist crunchy sounds.

His balance is frail.

His body seems to be leaning too far to the right, then too far to the left.

And there are his eyes. Lately, everything around him hangs in haze. He blinks without pause in an effort to clear what seems to him a glutinous film over existence.

If he concentrates on one clay foot, then the other, on one quavering hand, then the other, he discovers things begin to happen.

The floor steadily falls away.

The black lozenge grows larger.

He hears himself humming and concludes he must be happy.

The tune is familiar.

Give it a second.

Give it a second.

Yes: the piece for chorus and orchestra he composed himself—*Hymn to Life*, the one he meant to be sung one day in commemoration of his accomplishments, a solemn audience grieving the profundity lost in their midst. Friedrich has to admit he still sustains a shudder of exhilaration whenever he hears it. How, at the conclusion, the A-sharp alleviates him, forms a sonic bridge to the satisfying decisiveness of the final phrasings.

The moral contrariety of that note has caused him on more than one occasion to shed a tear.

In the attic, the prospect is all amiss.

Friedrich expected a tight crawl space. Instead, the obscurity creates the sense of extensiveness, even after he has given himself time to adjust to the staggering lack of light. He cannot distinguish any walls and he cannot distinguish a single storage trunk or crate. He could just as well be standing in an open pasture beneath a starless night sky, except for the fragrance of warm dust and mold spores suspended in the air.

In any event, it is equally likely this is a Wednesday, of which he is no fonder than Tuesday.

He plans for a while.

Tentatively slides his left foot out in front of him and pokes around with his toe. When he encounters no resistance, he extends his right arm—first straight ahead, then into the blank above him.

Nothing.

Shoring up his courage, he shuffles forward half a meter.

The word for what he is doing, he recollects, is *groping*.

He is *groping* through the attic.

The floorboards seem solid enough, the atmosphere no hotter than below. This place consists of shades of very dark gray and very dark grayer like a three-dimensional slate pencil drawing.

If it isn't Wednesday, no doubt it is Thursday.

Friday at the latest.

Friday, Saturday, or Sunday.

He holds both arms ahead of him like a hypnotist mesmerizing his assistant and progresses with feet wide apart, the sound of his shuffling reminding him of a straw broom sweeping unhurriedly across the planks beneath him.

Without music, he thinks, humming to himself, life would be a mistake. Music has always enabled him to master a mood without reflection. Its syntax exists in a different register from the syntax of written words. Every key is a different emotion, every chord a means of experiencing experience with less deliberation.

Sitting at the piano, inventing, the only thing he could ever hold in his mind was the last measure he played.

Notes are beautiful sparrows in a snowstorm.

The curious thing about this present place is the sense of— *openness* is the word: the sense of *openness* to it. Friedrich gropes forward for what seems like two or three minutes without coming into contact with a single object.

What good is an attic if there is nothing in it?

He suddenly grows bored and resolves to retrace his steps.

The problem when he turns around is he cannot determine where the ladder should be: he anticipates seeing a fountain of light flooding up from the floor, only everything remains very dark gray and very dark grayer.

He stops, hum trailing off, and tries to get his bearings, revolves, sets forth on a new path. Presses forward, groping, knowing at times like this his bladder invariably starts loading with apprehension, at which instant his bladder starts loading with apprehension. The need to piss unwinds into a distinct, stubborn fact.

He comes to another halt, shaken, resigned, and, standing there, believes he can make out a glimmer far ahead of him.

Off he goes at a speedy shuffle.

Friedrich has smote history into two halves.

Surely he can hold his fluids another few seconds.

Except.

Except it isn't the ladder at all. The light seems to be emanating from some sort of crack in the wall separating this part of
the attic from another, or perhaps this part of the attic from the
exterior of the building. No: it is the outline of a door.

A door?

A door.

And so when Friedrich reaches it he extends a delicate white
hand and fumbles for the latch.

Next he is in a train compartment and out the window the northern Italian countryside is scudding past in a browngreen smudge.

Across from him, Lou rests her head on her mother's shoulder, napping. Frau Salomé surveys the hills wobbling by from beneath her feathered hat. Beside him, Rée is reading a Swiss newspaper.

It is early May. It is 1882. It was childish and it was naïve and
yet the reality remains that Friedrich loved Lou instantly and loved
Lou completely.

When he cornered Rée in the hallway, asking him to propose on his behalf, Rée hesitated, but Friedrich was persistent. Rée
relented in the end. He promised Friedrich he would approach
Fräulein Salomé after dinner that evening.

The rest of the afternoon ached, overfull with minutes. Friedrich sat at his writing table and observed the ochre smog condens-
ing above Rome. He rose and dressed in his best suit. He took his
seat again. He consulted the watch on the end of his fob. He rose
and paced the room. He took his seat again. He rose and combed
out his mustache. He went down to the dining room to take up his
position behind his chair.

During the meal, he could neither bring himself to glance at
Lou nor contribute to the conversation and, afterward, he returned
to his room and began to pack. He had made a fool of himself.

He would leave first thing in the morning. He would apologize to Malwida for his abrupt departure and he would leave first thing in the morning.

There was a knock on the door.

Friedrich raised his head. He thought better of answering. He had done enough damage already. It would take him years to live this down. When he was finished packing he would apologize to Malwida for his abrupt departure and apologize to Rée for putting him in such an awkward position and he would leave first thing in the morning.

There was another knock.

Conversely.

Conversely, one had to see things through. One had to fight every war to its conclusion, no matter what that conclusion might be. This was the definition, after all, of noblesse and philosophy.

A third knock followed, louder than the first two, and Friedrich wasn't so much walking toward the door as he was sidling up on it as if it might fly off its hinges and levitate before him.

Lou was waiting in the hallway, hands clasped neatly before her, features unreadable.

Would it be possible for her to come in for a moment? she asked.

Friedrich examined his shoes. A good polish certainly couldn't hurt. He examined Lou's shoes. Her feet were outrageously small. It made his seem like they had been surgically detached from an elephant and sewn on below his ankle joints.

He stepped away from the entrance and offered her a seat at his writing desk. She took it. He remained standing. He noticed Lou was talking. She was talking and she was telling him something. She was talking and she was telling him how genuinely flattered she had been by his kind proposition. She thought of him, as she was sure he already knew, in the highest possible terms.

If not a full polish, then at least the application of a damp cloth was in order. This would at minimum eliminate some grime, some scuffing.

What would people think of him?

And yet, Lou was saying, her voice smooth and confident, she was afraid she had to confess she did not conceive of Friedrich as a husband. She did not conceive of anyone in those terms. Rather, she had always been and always would be committed to living the independent life, a life unburdened by such constraints as marriage.

Or, Friedrich thought, he could throw them out, or give them to a filthy beggar on the filthy street if Friedrich could in actual fact find a filthy beggar on the filthy street willing to take these leather monstrosities off his hands.

And yet, Lou was saying, she would like to respond to his generous proposal with a counterproposal of her own: would there be any chance he might consider joining Rée and her in Vienna?

Friedrich filched a glance in her direction.

Their plan was to live together, she said, study together, keep each other productive company. Lou realized the instant she picked up Friedrich's treatise on power just how much he had to teach her. Would he be so kind as to give her idea some serious consideration? He needn't answer this very minute, of course, but if he might at least agree to mull it over at his convenience, she would be ever so grateful.

And so here they are on a train clattering through the Italian countryside: Lou napping, her mother scowling, Rée reading, Friedrich watching.

They have decided to holiday in northern Italy and southern Switzerland for another week or ten days, refreshing their spirits, then aim for the Austrian capital where they will search for a house in which to settle.

Out the window, a lake shines like a tin plate.

A skinny boy on a bicycle stops on the dusty road paralleling the tracks. He dismounts, lets his bicycle fall to his feet. It appears as if he has just become aware of something remarkable in the pallid sky above him. His arms hang at his sides. His mouth opens.

He is there.

He is not there.

Friedrich cranes his neck, trying to see what the boy was looking at with such avidity, but, unsuccessful, turns back to the compartment, feeling the sudden urge to pass water.

He rises, excuses himself with a demure bow, and extends a delicate white hand to release the latch on the door leading to the cramped corridor beyond.

A light autumn drizzle is falling around him in a cobblestone courtyard.

There is something in his right hand.

He looks down and is surprised to learn he is clutching a dueling sword. A young unhandsome man with undersized lips and oversized ears standing opposite him is holding one as well. The safety tips, Friedrich notes, have been removed.

En garde, his friend Deussen announces calmly by his side, and the unhandsome man lunges.

It is Bonn. It is 1864. Friedrich enrolled at the university less than a month ago and from the outset his goal has been to be one of the boys. He has had enough thinking, enough solitude. He was a good student at Pforta, mind you, but never a sensation, never anybody about whom his teachers said *keep an eye on that one, he's going to surprise us someday*, and so all he wants now is to be part of the party. He wants to enjoy an average stay at an average university before he moves out into the average world to become an average…what, exactly?

An average teacher, possibly.

Teaching is a perfectly honorable profession.

Except from the outset he hasn't had a particularly easy time of it, not knowing what constitutes average enjoyment. He studied those around him and even tried to carry on a flirtation with Deussen's sister for five days until she asked her brother to tell Friedrich to stay away from her. He much prefers cream cakes to beer. Of cream cakes he could eat any number.

Last week Deussen talked him into joining one of the student unions and Friedrich reluctantly agreed and tonight they have been out drinking with some fraternity chums.

On their unsteady drift home, the group bumped into another from a rival fraternity with whom they began talking. Someone suggested the time had come for dueling scars and Friedrich heard himself agreeing. It began to drizzle. Seven or eight of them are now in a courtyard and a young unhandsome man with undersized lips and oversized ears is lunging at Friedrich with a sword. Friedrich lunges, too, forgetting in his enthusiasm to raise his weapon.

The battle lasts four seconds and then there is lightning at the bridge of his nose. Friedrich is lying on his back in a puddle in the long wool overcoat his mother gave him as a going-away present, wicking like a human washcloth. His eyes are closed, people are snickering around him, and Deussen is standing over him.

Fritz? Deussen is saying. Fritz? Are you in there, Fritz?

A camera's flash powder ignites, the studio around him cramming with shadowless dazzle.

Friedrich goes momentarily sightless.

It is mid-May. It is 1882. It is Lucerne. Friedrich, Rée, and Lou have decided to document their stay by visiting the popular Swiss photographer, Jules Bonnet, while, under the weather, Frau Salomé has opted to remain behind in her hotel room.

Another, perhaps? he hears a voice ask from beyond the light rage.

Yes! Lou's voice responds brightly. Another! Another!

The set design is Friedrich's choice: a screen depicting the brooding Alps under an ominous sky before which squats a low-slung wooden peasant cart. Lou has assumed the role of teamster in the cart's bed. Rée and Friedrich stand in for the mules.

Rée excuses himself and slips outside to roll a quick cigarette while bereted Bonnet and his pasty assistant set up for the next shot.

Friedrich, feeling a transient joy about the arrangement of the current variation, sees an opening. He asks Lou if he might talk to her briefly in private. They step into the adjoining sitting room. The burgundy walls are muddled with Bonnet's photographs. The leather sofa is too big by half. Without delay, Friedrich proposes a second time.

They have had several weeks now to make each other's acquaintance more fully, he suggests. Is Lou wholly, entirely, utterly convinced she hasn't perhaps had a change of heart?

Lou gently, simply, declines him again.

The small sitting room becomes very large.

Friedrich and Lou examine each other for three downbeats, hunting for something neither of them can find, and then Friedrich is apologizing for the inconvenience he has just caused her. He doesn't know what came over him. He is a clown. Is it conceivable, is it in his dreams possible to hope, that some day she will find it within herself to pardon such unseemliness on his part?

Lou is talking to him. Lou is saying something. Lou is telling him to think nothing of it. She continues to hold his friendship in the highest regard. He may doubt many things in the world, but he should never doubt that.

Friedrich apologizes for his apology. He is deeply disappointed in himself. He should have known better. It is entirely his fault.

He will leave this very afternoon.

Lou is talking to him. Lou is saying something. Lou is telling him they should put it all behind them. Let them persist in their plans. Let them carry on with their expedition. They are all, in the end, having a splendid time, are they not?

Out of words, out of energy, Friedrich closes his eyes and waits in the enlarging room for this incident to shift into the past tense.

Lou reaches up and runs the back of her hand down his cheek, pivots, and disappears through the door leading back into the studio.

Friedrich remains behind.

He sets about collecting himself. It could have been worse. She could have laughed at him. She could have kissed him. She could have walked out in a huff. She could have kissed him. Friedrich collects himself, eyes closed, shame clenching his head.

When he finally returns to the studio, Lou and Rée are waiting for him.

He cannot decide whether it is obvious they are sharing a secret or only appears obvious they are sharing a secret.

Positions, if you please, bereted Bonnet announces.

Lou steps up into the cart and kneels. She is wearing her wasp-waisted black dress with the white lace trim. She looks directly into the lens. Rée stands in front of the cart, also facing the camera straight on, his right hand under his jacket, Napoleanesque, trace of grin still on his lips. Friedrich in his frock coat poses behind and to the left of Rée, body leaning back five degrees, staring off at something stage left, as if slightly surprised or vaguely puzzled by what he sees. At the last possible instant, an idea wells up in him and he starts.

A minute, he says, stepping out of the frame. A minute, if I may...

Bonnet clucks and looks up from behind his equipment like a prairie dog and his pasty assistant exhales a liter of air. Friedrich rummages in the prop trunk until he finds what he is looking for and returns carrying a makeshift whip fashioned from a stick, some rope, and a sprig of artificial lilacs. Stepping back into the frame, he presents his gift to Lou.

There is more breathing.

Rée looks at Friedrich looks at Bonnet looks at his assistant looks at Lou who raises the whip in her right hand, visibly delighted by this gesture of trespass, eyes penetrating, face unexpectedly hard.

Rée's grin widens almost indiscernibly.

Friedrich turns and faces the perplexing prospect.

Say *Deutschland, Deutschland über alles,* Bonnet instructs, dipping behind his equipment again, and pressing the camera's trigger.

Flash.

7 p.m.

Except I am not there.

I am here.

I am, that is, more than a little secure in the notion I am lying on my back in a damp bed, swaying, head cradled in an old woman's lap.

Fredericus Caesar has sicked himself again.

The ludicrous diversity of his ailments: if nothing else, they prove the human body evinces a sense of humor.

This female sharing my oxygen smells like grandmothers who don't get out enough. She is occupied with the use of sounds. My breath is aromatic with dog droppings.

She wipes off the curdling egesta from Caesar's person with a moist washrag.

Here is a secret: she enjoys extraordinary strength and cunning.

When I am not looking, she often vials behavior water into my food, into my drink, sprinkles it over my privates as I sleep. And then Caesar can't sing. Theseus goes on holiday.

Math is out of the question.

Where are we again? I hear all the voices asking.

The maid apes a servant aping compassion, dabbing at my chin and cheeks, and occupies herself with the use of sounds.

I am, she tells me, in a city called Weimar in a building called the Nietzsche Archive at the portal to a new century. The lower floors are fussy with memorials to me and manuscripts by me and photographs of me and my snaky walking stick. The upper floor is fussy with me. It takes a whole room and veranda to lodge the last god.

I am sorry I invented it, by the way, the human race.

The perspective of the room tilts. Weight rushes from behind my forehead. Stunningly, I am buoyed up, propped against her big sloppy breasts. I struggle briefly, try to struggle briefly, but she hangs on hard and, winded, I resolve to concentrate on breathing instead.

There is an attempt to drown me in shaving foam.

There is an attempt to scald me with boiling water.

A razor blade intimidates the corners of my vision.

Fredericus sicks himself again, this time on the back of her wrist. Another wet rag slaps in. A comb made of pins. A brush made of barbed wire. A hand mouses beneath his hospital gown and yanks my penis as if it were the lead plug at the bottom of a bell cord.

Fredericus goes away.

He visits an October morning in Leipzig.

Lou and Rée and he are on their way to Paris. The previous night they stayed up past two in his hotel room, drinking bricky wine, laughing, provoking each other to think closer to the brink. Fredericus paraded back and forth in front of them lounging on the still-made bed, drunk on the elation of tribe.

When he woke the next morning, Lou and Rée were gone.

Fredericus was lying on the floor, stormy head beneath an askew sofa.

He rose cautiously, slipped on his robe, stepped into the hall, and knocked on Lou and her mother's door.

No answer.

He eased himself down the corridor and tried Rée's room.

More nothing.

He descended to the front desk to ask after his friends, and a man with the annoying habit of letting his plump tongue poke out of his mouth when he wasn't speaking told him they had left at dawn. Fredericus told him he was wrong. Lou and Rée and Frau Salomé were at breakfast. They were out for a stroll.

No, the man with the floppy tongue said. They had called for a coach and left for the station with their bags in tow. The sun had barely thought itself into being as they pulled away from the hotel entrance.

Fredericus ascended the stairs to his room, threw on his clothes, and hurried out into the streets where he spent that morning and afternoon roaming the gray city center like a cat left out in a blizzard.

On his way back to the hotel at dusk, he stopped by the train station and bought a ticket to Basel and from Basel to Genoa. From Genoa he would take a coach to Rapallo. At Rapallo, he would become invisible.

On his way back to the hotel at dusk, he ducked into an

apothecary and bought a measure of opium. That night his sleep turned into winter earth.

Is it possible to die of memory?

Yes: anything is possible.

And so I effect the great extravagance, the opening of my eyes, like this…yes…and find myself propped among pillows and dressed in a burgundy silk robe with black velvet trim. Fredericus smells like soap, peppermint, and clean sheets. At the foot of my boat bed stands my sister with her coarse hands on her wide hips.

She evaluates the situation like a captain his battlefield. Her short curly colorless hair looks like a man's bad rug. Her lips look as thin and straight as a compass needle.

Fredericus uses his mind to cross the room and crawl behind her face.

It is like peering through a pink-skin mask. The first thing he comes to understand about her is that she believes smiling is a weakness of musculature. The second thing he comes to understand is that the ghoul spilled in the bed before her has hijacked his soul.

Both women become occupied with the use of sounds. But not at him.

Does this mean I will perhaps be home soon? he asks in the fullness of time.

Because he is not here anymore because he is there.

He is using his mind to stand at the window. The curtains are pulled back. Four immense orange suns hang in the sky above the trees.

The last coruscations of daylight above the city.

And then they are dying.

And then they are dying some more.

And then they are dead.

tongue

There is lightning at the bridge of your nose and your friend Deussen is talking above you only you have already lost interest in what he is saying. You are thinking rather about how the tongue bleeding in your mouth is not your tongue. You have suspected as much for years. It is a stranger's tongue the tongue of an animal and you remember waking in the middle of the night to hear it practicing the mimicry of vowels it heard while you were awake and as far as you are concerned it shouldn't be referred to as a *tongue* no but as *the error beneath your palate*. One day in the future you imagine waking to find it lumped on the bloody pillow beside your head and a fresh glistening muscle thriving in the white cage of your dentition.

One day sitting at your writing desk in your flat down the road from the old Basel gate you will look at the pages of the manuscript on which you are working and grasp with resounding disappointment that the architecture of every phrase is wrong your house of signs a ruin not the *what* of saying the *how*. You will look at the sheet of paper in front of you and all you will see is how every blocky paragraph is the color of ashes just another sentence in a language busy with them. You should have been composing with wind because every writer in your country has become a journalist and for them words are panes of glass through which to see how cows move in unison when you clap your hands and in the next breath it will come to you writing isn't expansion but compression a texturing into fragment saying in seven sentences what everyone else says in a book saying in seven sentences what everyone else *doesn't* say in a book employing the figure of aphorism because you do not want to be read but learned by heart and this is how you will construct a particle philosophy for a particulate world bringing together what is shard and riddle and chance engineering with your flesh and from that day forward this will be what you will mean when you say the word *tongue*.

historia abscondita

The term for what he is doing, Friedrich recollects, is *groping*.

He is *groping* through the attic, wide-gaited, barefoot, continuing from time to time to reach down and scratch his tailbone through his hospital gown even though the itch has long since dispersed.

He has been at it now, he would guess, for more than an hour. His skin is oily with heat. His rowdy hair clings to his forehead and cheekbones as if an Italian fisherman had draped a baby black octopus over his pate. He is lost. He is lonely. This unlit space seems to unravel without cessation.

It must be what Christians imagine when they imagine life

without their great conjecture: something tarrishly thick and dark, immeasurable, abandoned.

Friedrich is positive, groping, he is no fonder of Friday than he is of Thursday or Wednesday, Tuesday or Saturday, Sunday or Monday, although he is reasonably sure he must have been born on one of these.

Give it a second.

Give it a second.

Yes, that's it: October fifteenth.

Of this he is virtually certain he is virtually certain, since he seems to recall he shares the date with his namesake the Prussian king, yes, and the Roman versifier Publius Vergilius Maro born in…born in…the same day in any event in seventeen-something-something that Edward Gibbon, sitting among the remains of the Roman Capitol, conceived the plan to write his big book about damage and culture, and Thomas Hastings, the nearsighted American albino with a hankering for catchy hymns, was born in seventeen-something-something-else.

On the same morning, but in a wholly different year, Napoleon commenced his exile on the rock named St. Helena in the blustery South…and…

Friedrich's fingertips brush brick and he pulls up short.

Brick or rock or rough wood. It is tricky to tell which in this total eclipse. A coarse, charcoalish material, in any case. He has been holding his arms out ahead of him, testing the light's absence with his hands, and here is a brick or rock or rough wood…what?

Friedrich runs a palm along the surface.

A wall.

Yes, that's it: a wall.

Friedrich commences sidling along it, feeling.

The brick or rock or rough wood extends one meter. It extends two. It extends three.

Making progress, his chest cavity swells with optimism: follow the wall around, and in the end Friedrich is sure he will arrive at the beginning.

Far off, suspended in a pale gray nimbus, he sees himself as a young man, barely twenty-two, sitting across from his mother and sister on the veranda after dinner one evening, asking out of the blue:

What is the point, what specifically is the point, of considering the Scriptures with a slovenly eye while bringing all the resources of scholarship and historical criticism to bear on Greek and Roman texts? I'm just curious.

It is 1866. It is April. It is Naumburg.

Friedrich is home from university for Easter.

Why choose to study Christianity in the first place, he continues, just curious, when one is presented with an array of other religions one could choose to study instead? Wasn't each of them finally as equally attractive, as equally felt by their followers, and as equally hollow a product of a people's childhood as the one with the bogeyman deity who loaded crossbows for the Crusades and assembled racks for the Inquisition? It's just a question. I was just wondering.

His mother smiles at him with affection.

Lisbeth parts her lips to argue.

Friedrich presses on, light-headed and restless.

Correct me if I'm wrong, but wasn't he the only authentic Christian who ever lived, Friedrich asks, just curious, that decadent Jew with the pathologically excitable nervous system sent down to earth to save humanity from his pathologically excitable father? And wasn't the upshot the intellectual and spiritual contamination of hundreds of generations to come? Christ may have been Plato's fault, of course, but weren't Descartes, Locke, Kant, and the rest Christ's? Look at doubting René standing on a street corner in

Stockholm, vowing to suspect everything, and then offering proofs of God's existence. Look at Oxford John citing chapter and verse to prove his empiricism. Look at the Königsberg clock-setter translating the Messiah into the gabble of German idealism.

Friedrich's mother smiles, knuckles distending her cheek, right up to his announcement that he will no longer be attending Easter services at an institution which propagates superstitions. Then Franziska's soft white hands lift to fidget in Franziska's soft bunned hair, and Lisbeth launches her own assault against her brother's apostasy, and Friedrich feels both superior and cornered. He tells them the will to a system is the lack of integrity. He tells them life, real life, is a refusal to be governed. He tells them to be fretful and multiply. Lisbeth's voice rises, Friedrich's voice rises, and Franziska flutters into the house, her soft white hands fidgeting.

An hour later Friedrich finds himself hunched in a horse-drawn cab on his way back to the station and back to university, stomach hurting, blue flame sputtering behind his eyes.

The remains of his family slowly falling away behind him.

Little white figures on a train track at dusk, dropping farther and farther into the past, unable to catch up no matter how hard they run.

His palm is reading brick or rock or rough wood and then it is reading air.

Friedrich stalls.

The wall is there.

The wall is not there.

He takes one step back, extends his arms, plays blindman's buff. And vacancy. Friedrich makes up his mind to wander out in a slow nautilus until he reconnects with solid matter, and starts, palming daytime nighttime, but soon the spiraling leads him to lose any sense of direction he might once have nearly possessed.

He is back on the foggy Lake Lucerne, drifting.

Before, the concept of pissing had existed for him within a general category of Needs to be Met in the Near Future. Now it pushes to the front of his consciousness with tidal urgency.

He sighs and he stops. He capitulates and, painstakingly, he hoists his hospital gown. Painstakingly, he eases himself down on his crunchy knees into a girlish squat.

Friedrich closes his eyes.

Friedrich relaxes his sphincter.

And nil: the liquid throb grows in intensity, but he can't bring forth a drop.

Friedrich Nietzsche understands with teeming clarity he will die this way, squatting here, gown raised, by himself.

He strains.

He strains some more.

Eventually he raises his right hand and massages his belly, turns that hand into a fist, throws a weak punch at his offending organs.

Unconvincingly, Friedrich begins beating himself up.

When he rises again, he is on the Piazza Carlo Alberto in front of the building where he rents a flat from the newsvendor Fino.

Friedrich fell in love with how the architect of this place confused inside with outside and erected a monument to sunshine. How the skylight ceiling floods the interior courtyard with luminous hope. How, when you look north up almost any nearby street on a clear day, you will catch a glimpse of the Alps levitating like a superimposed image in a photograph.

Except today is not a clear day.

Today the sky resembles a sheet of soiled linen.

Friedrich assesses it and reports aloud that it is the city's dry air that works its magic at this time of year: there is something exhilarating about the very act of breathing.

A blocky scarfed woman with her net shopping bag steps into the cobblestone street to avoid him.

It is Turin. It is 1889. Heinrich Hertz has just proved the breeze alive with radio waves, while the Parisians are busy employing two-and-a-half million rivets to build an iron nightmare for the Universal Exposition.

Still, Friedrich wishes the sky were bluer.

Everything points to rain. Rain or snow. He can't decide which would be more disheartening.

Either way, he has forgotten his tie.

It is early January and he has forgotten his tie and forgotten his shirt.

One reason for such obvious oversights may well in due course turn out to be that the epitaph on Descartes's tombstone reads *He lived well who hid well*, another that there are trilingual bookshops nearby.

The high-arched arcades comprising the pride of Turin extend over ten thousand meters through the city center. One can stroll them for hours and never pass the same phantom twice. In the excellent trattoria, the waiters treat Herr Professor Nietzsche most courteously. A pot of glorious coffee for only twenty centimes. Ice cream of the highest quality for thirty. In Turin, one does not pay a tip.

On the way out of his flat, Friedrich examined himself in the mirror and was elated to discover how fit he looked. His dark eyes sparked with vigor. His curtain mustache never appeared more magisterial.

Homo litteratus made flesh, looking ten years younger than he is.

Turin's vast squares, the duomo ducking in and out of sight, the gardens at the city's heart, the tree-line boulevards, the River

Po: this place is a hundred times more congenial than that chalky, treeless, stupid stretch of Riviera he is annoyed at himself for having been so long in putting behind him.

Here, the pulse is echt Swiss, existence worth living in every respect.

Only how did he miss the fact that he wasn't wearing a shirt? The tie he can understand. These things happen. But his beautiful lilac shirt?

His overcoat is apparently lacking as well.

He notices this when he notices he has begun shivering.

One reason for such obvious oversights may well in due course turn out to be that his room holds the *best* position in the center of the building: glorious light from early morning until late afternoon, and a charming view onto the Palazzo Carignano and the Carlo Alberto.

Given the evidence of his senses, it is already early January. There has yet to be a single knock on his door save for Fino the landlord come to collect his rent. On Christmas Day, Friedrich sat at his writing desk, hands spread out on the waxed surface before him, waiting very quietly.

Perhaps this is a function of his flat holding the *best* position in the center of the building, and perhaps it is a function of it costing only twenty-five francs a month, with service and a piano. In the evenings, he performs Wagner. Let people say what they will. Richard's early efforts are still the only authentic music. Perhaps it would be unwise to admit such a thing in print these days, but there you have it. Zarathustra has seen to it that Turin has been Siegfriedized.

Friedrich lowers his hands, extracts his notebook and pencil, and opens the former.

Mouth agape, he tries to catch the circumfluous thoughts of passersby.

He nudges his spectacles up on his nose and, holding his notebook close to his face so there will be no cheating, he carefully composes:

1. Persist in becoming invisible.
2. Memorandum to high courts of Europe suggesting anti-German league.
3. Traverse the Rubicon and sing a new song.
4. Italian being the language that consistently sounds either disappointed or argumentative.
5. Shoot history of mankind into smithereens.
6.

Except.

Except this is all wrong, he announces to no one, glancing up, drawn to the unfamiliar noise across the square.

A gathering of horse-drawn cabs, steam chewing the animals' heads. In one, a brawny driver standing on his seat, bringing his whip down on his tired nag while his colleagues continue about their business.

A woman in a black veil situates herself in a nearby rig. Its driver clucks. Its mare clops forward.

A man in a derby exits a café, biting into a donut.

It is about to rain or snow or sleet or hail or ice over and there is a cabbie beating a horse and the horse's spine is curved in like a loose washline and there is only so much one human can take. The driver's pudgy face is red. His hat has fallen off because he is striking the animal so hard. His arms are the diameter of Friedrich's thighs, his chest a Roman column, and yet the real problem, as Friedrich sees it, putting away his notebook and pencil and stepping into the street, is not that the horse won't move. The real problem is the horse cannot move, and there is only so much one being can take.

How, for instance, can a person call each wholly unique green object that grows in a tree a *leaf?*

One reason for such obvious oversights may well in due course turn out to be that everywhere the powers are whispering, the breeze alive with radio waves, but it is difficult to discern what they are going on about, another that the cobblestones seem solid enough beneath his shoes as he begins to trot, but this will always remain a matter of some conjecture.

Three bloody strips appear along the nag's back like long lovely holiday ribbons.

Friedrich trots faster.

His arms no longer seem to bend at the elbows.

It is about to rain or snow or sleet or hail or ice over and there is only so much one human can take and then Friedrich finds himself in front of the cab, pointing accusingly at the driver and shouting: *This isn't happening!*

He points accusingly at the swaybacked horse and shouts: *This isn't happening!*

He floats his finger across the buildings lining the street, the herd of people slowing and starting to stare, the inconsiderate sky itself, and he shouts it again, as if explaining a truism everyone around him should already understand but seems somehow to be missing. Get it right, and everything will be fine. Get it right, and Zarathustra can stop in at the café for breakfast on his way home.

The pudgy-faced cabbie looks down at him, appraising, then shrugs an Italian shrug and laughs and raises his whip for another lash and Friedrich has fallen forward before he knows this is what he is going to do, arms around the animal's neck, eyes squinched shut. The world collapses away from him. Then he is enjoying the close-up bitter scent of horsehide because this is what the future smells like: like Paul Rée climbing over the banister of the bridge on which he and Lou used to talk for hours and leaping into the night a dozen years below. The way the black water absorbs him. The way he suddenly becomes wreckage.

Friedrich, eyes squinched shut, decides he appreciates the clamor of the crowd forming around him.

He appreciates the radio waves enlivening the air and enjoys knowing Fino will take good care of him because Schopenhauer once said you should treat a work of art like a prince and let it speak to you first and so we are finally getting somewhere.

Friedrich listens to the frayed wind tunnel blowing beneath the horse's bones and when he begins to hear the powers inside clarify themselves he is so thankful he lifts his face just enough to deliver a single modest kiss.

second part:
on the spirit of gravity

8 p.m.

Is he awake? someone asks.

Someone asks am I awake and there is a gap in the expenditure of sound, then my sister's voice answers, saying:

It is sometimes difficult to establish his state with any certainty.

I am being watched.

It feels not unpleasant.

Someone other than the first someone says something I don't quite catch and next my sister is employing language again:

When Herr Professor Nietzsche undertakes one of his metaphysical voyages, he often leaves his body behind in a condition of repose.

The enigmatic face, another comments. The leonine aura. Do you imagine he is cognizant of our presence?

It is as if, a third voice says, his soul were gazing beyond the limits of infinity, endlessly distant from human affairs.

It is, Lisbeth agrees. My brother has traveled to planes we bodybound cannot imagine. He has spoken of endless light and minds above minds merging without the encumbrance of mortal fabric. The beings inhabiting this Golgotha of Absolute Spirit speak to us in our dreams. When babies die, this is where they go.

My llama is very good.

I part my lips and close them, trouty, trying to join in on the conversation.

Look! one of the voices blurts out. He is speaking to us...

He is speaking beyond us, Lisbeth corrects. If we are fortunate, perhaps we shall overhear part of the exchange. Herr Professor Steiner—you inquired earlier about his condition of advanced awareness. I remember my dear mother once asserting my brother had turned his back on the injurious nihilism ruling his middle years and reestablished his nourishing relationship with God Beyond God. I have no reason to believe otherwise. Herr Professor Nietzsche's final volume of thoughts and meditations, which as you know I am currently editing with Herr Gast, will, I am quite sure, prove as much.

A long assimilation of sister data.

We are speaking of nothing less, then, the reverent expenditure elucidates, than the beginnings of an original mode of psychic perception...

I am a simple woman, Herr Professor Steiner, and yet I find myself firmly convinced that what we are witnessing is the inception of a new evolutionary stage in understanding.

A resurrection of consciousness...

Breathing, I say, interrupting them.

All the pigeons wing home. Shutters are fastened against the storm. I take a short rest, regain my strength, and push forward.

Breathing, I say, *in the end doesn't work.*

Children clear the streets. Dolphins die. There is all of this to think, again and again.

My sister believes my referring to her for five and a half decades as the animal that squirts half-digested fodder at its adversary is an expression of endearment on my part.

I, therefore, can no longer endorse the philosophy of Eternal Recurrence: it might force me to reencounter my family.

A resurrection of consciousness, she affirms. This is precisely what our scientific research points toward. Although I should of course emphasize that it is still in its nascent stages. And, I am sorry to report (her voice modulates from major to minor key, arriving at a four-bar rest to provide emphasis for the adagio that follows) we are in continual need of generosity on the part of others to carry forth with our mission. I think it is fair to say, however, that what we see before us today is the first example of a new race for a new Germany.

There are more vocalizations.

Where, I wonder, are my party favors?

We must keep this essential inquiry alive, the reverent expenditure replies. I can assure you my Anthroposophical Society will be honored to support such study. Furthermore, I should think there would be those at the highest levels in our current government who would be only too happy to do the same.

Your munificence is overwhelming, my llama says, all flattery. The Nietzsche Archive owes you an immense debt of gratitude.

Not at all, Frau Förster. Not at all. The gratitude is all mine.

May I suggest, she suggests, we carry on our discussion downstairs in the sitting room—over perhaps a nice cup of tea or small glass of schnapps? I believe the servant is awaiting our pleasure...

stomach

You knock on Wagner's door thirty-some-odd years before and it is just past eight and raining violently and you are under the impression you have been invited to a musical soirée but your father answers and from what you can tell he is alone. He is tall and slim and dressed in Wagner's outlandish Dutch painter's costume chocolate velvet jacket knee-breeches silk stockings buckled shoes Rembrandt beret blue cravat. Behind him the hall is empty lit by a single candle and he looks over your shoulder as if expecting someone more important to come up the walkway and so you look too but there is no one and you are wearing a shabby suit because it is the best you can afford. Your tongue is not your tongue and your teeth not your teeth you are borrowing them from a very sick man who barely hangs on to life in someone else's imagination. You have come to meet Wagner who wants to make the acquaintance of the bright young philologist he heard so much about during a recent visit to Basel only you find yourself facing your father. *Giving birth* he tells you with great affection while looking over your shoulder *is the production of proof concerning the parents' inadequacies* and then he turns his back on you and wanders down the silent empty hall and you hesitate before following. He leads you to an elegant drawing room slightly larger than a closet where there are no windows or perhaps they have been covered over with the satin wallpaper and it is very dark your stomach hurts a large stuffed leather chair and miniature grand piano atop which rests another candle comprising the only furniture. It is so confined the air so heavy with Wagner's patchouli perfume it is difficult to draw a breath and your father indicates the chair and you sit his back still to you and address him with a few words of respect telling him he looks extremely good for a dead man you miss him very much. You remember you say how he was liked and welcomed everywhere for his conversation and kindness and your father moves away and hunches down at the miniature piano knees up by his ears and speaks quickly cutting you off telling you if he had lived he would be the same age Wagner is now and please open your mouth. His back is to you and he bangs out several parts from the *Meistersinger* imitating each voice with great exuberance then stops sharply leaps off the bench opens it rummages inside comes up with a manuscript so fat it could never have fit in there except it has Wagner's autobiography. He sits again back to you and begins reading and every few sentences interrupts himself to tell you to please open your mouth. You tell him you miss him very much and the first five years of your life the years he was alive were your happiest and you ask does he recall that Saturday morning he said it is time to learn how to fish and took you on horseback into the countryside you sat in front of him in the saddle balancing his rod and tackle and everything was true the sun feeling like when you crouch directly in front of a fireplace on a winter's night no he does not your stomach hurts he continues reading interrupting himself every few sentences and telling you to please open your mouth. He is not you realize before long reading about Wagner's past but about Wagner's future telling you how Wagner will in time come to exhibit the Christian pathology. Your father winces when he pronounces these words. *Be careful* he says *they're hot.* After *Parsifal* Wagner's work will bloat with hysterical women and its flesh drop off and it will turn sticky then histrionic then pretentious. *He that humbleth himself* your father says *wants to be exalted.* He winces and is on his feet again agitated the pages of the manuscript scattered across the floor as if a heavy wind has blown through the room and he is standing next to your chair his back still to you but he reaches out behind him and discovers your face and feels along its contours as if he were sightless. When he reaches your lips he strokes them with his forefinger and gently slips a digit between them and tells you to please open your mouth you hesitate he pushes a little you instinctively resist and then he is prying your jaws apart forcing his first three fingers between your upper and lower front teeth. You ask him to stop try to ask him but your mouth is full of him and he is touching each of your teeth as if every one were a beautiful pearl that could reverse time. He examines each with his fingers and you are progressively interested in his touch until he grips your left incisor with the strength of pliers and begins to unscrew it and you balk your hands shooting up to stop him but you are no match for his power the first tooth is already out the inside of your mouth bloody. His back is to you and your stomach hurts and he takes your tooth and raises it to his own mouth and you can see him huddle over it as he inserts it with a wet grinding sound like roots twisted in mud. He reaches behind him and begins to caress your lips again fingertips tickling and forces your jaws apart a second time his fingers eeling around inside your mouth searching for another tooth they choose an upper molar grasp it unscrew it then that one is in him too. He repeats this gesture twenty times and afterward turns around his mouth smeared with your blood your gums pocked with slimy holes and your father tells you to please open your mouth he has some difficulty articulating the words because of his new set of teeth he tells you to please open your mouth and when you do not he reaches out and runs a hand through your hair tenderly and then down the side of your face and when he reaches your lips pauses and three fingers are inside your mouth and you are having trouble taking air. He inserts three fingers inside your mouth and then four and then his whole fist and you are convinced your jaw muscles will tear your jawbone shatter you are gagging he is forcing his fist down your throat. He exerts steady insistent affectionate pressure and his pink-smeared lips are close to your right ear left arm braced against your chair for support. He exerts steady insistent affectionate pressure and his arm is up to the elbow inside you and the joint presents a temporary problem but your father braces himself against your chair and shoves with great vigor and then you feel his fingers wadding up your stomach sac from the inside and then his arm is slowly withdrawing and your stomach coming with it and your father is whispering *what I have given you I have come to take back what is yours has always been mine* and you listen with interest coming to appreciate this reclamation may take quite some time and so you attempt to settle into your chair make yourself comfortable trying and succeeding to love your father a little harder every second your consciousness remains intact.

by searching out origins
one becomes a crab

The cream cake is undoubtedly among Germany's most valuable contributions to Europe, Friedrich thinks, attempting to make himself comfortable inside the cramped tool shed at the back of his mother's cramped garden.

Lisbeth is standing in front of him in her Easter dress.

Impatiently.

It is April. It is 1859. It is Naumburg. France and Piedmont are at war with Austria. A new book by a British naturalist claims we are all in actual fact just monkeys with minds. Still, it is a holiday.

It is a holiday and it is warm and it is sunny and inside a furry bee is ticking against the cloudy windowpane.

The bee meanders away. Outside, bird diction is general. The bee returns.

A cart rattles and clops by in the lane and on the other side of the garden wall the cart's horse snorffles loudly.

Friedrich tries to contemplate the sugar, butter, the crumbly excellence of the cream cake, but finds himself instead imagining his mother moving through the hushed rooms in the house across the small stone patio.

Perhaps she is checking on Alwine's work.

In Friedrich's imagination, she is humming to herself distractedly, gliding through last year or the year before while he is busy preparing to step into tomorrow.

He tries not to imagine it that way, of course, yet can't help himself. He guiltily admits that, when he is away at boarding school and pictures her, he misses her terribly. But when he is home on holiday he feels almost nothing except the need to walk out the front door, and begin to travel beyond her, because no one returns from a trip the same person who left.

His need has something to do with the closed-off scent of number 18 Weingarten, like a quilt before spring airing, the motionlessness, how his mother wears the same plain dress month after month only to replace it with one almost identical to it.

Friedrich experiences a frothy sensation. Although his teachers at Pforta seem to consider him merely competent, industrious and conscientious among other industrious and conscientious students, he knows every evening in addition to his regular studies he composes poems, keeps a notebook, and performs experiments in the autobiographical essay until the blue phantoms begin to lap behind his eyelids and his vision smudges. These days he cannot stop thinking and feeling. Sometimes he sleeps only four or five hours a night. Pages and pages of ideas unspool from his forehead like Rapunzel's hair from her tower.

Friedrich knows most are boyishly trite, overstated and un-refined, a fourteen-year-old's insights prinked out in faux-adult phrasing and syntax. He is continually dissatisfied with who he is, what he has accomplished, and he longs to enter next year or the year after, yet next year or the year after are always happening somewhere else much more engaging.

Math is another story, needless to say.

Math and, oddly, modern languages.

The headmaster knocked on his door as he was packing for this visit and warned Friedrich in no uncertain terms that, if things did not change with respect to his dreadful arithmetic papers and change soon, it is quite possible Friedrich would never graduate, nor can he bring himself to believe completely the Italians and French and English don't secretly think in German.

Surely they dream in Greek.

Who doesn't?

But Friedrich can only do Shakespeare in translation, Vol-taire with an open dictionary on his desk, and you would think Italian is simply slurred Latin without the tangly declensions, al-though you would be entirely mistaken.

On the other side of the garden, Friedrich's past is gliding through the rooms of the butterscotch house with green shutters.

Lisbeth is standing in front of him here in the tool shed.

Impatiently.

An hour after lunch, she found him with a book on his bed (he almost never reads them cover to cover anymore, just thumbs through searching for passages that excite him) and told him she wanted to show him something, come along with her, and now her compass-needle lips are moving.

Friedrich thinks about cream cakes, attempting to make him-self comfortable in preparation for the future's arrival, only he is having an enormously difficult time of it. He pictures how a bite falls to pieces and melts on your tongue like a cube of bready ice, returning matter to Democritus, but his little sister is standing in front of him and he couldn't have envisioned things more differently and now his sister is saying *Come on.*

Come on, she is saying. Let me show you.

Her sandblond hair is arranged in pigtails, her Easter dress white with pale blue cornflowers dappled across it. Her eyes are the color of pewter. Most of us don't so much live life as get lived by it, Friedrich understands. He tries to remember to mention this finding to her later. At the moment, though, he is occupied with locating something worthy to say about the current circumstances.

I don't know, he responds.

Lisbeth appraises him for a very long time, then snorts.

Of course you don't, Fritz. You never know. Come on. Let me show you. Let me show you what I learned.

I don't feel so good. My stomach...

Lisbeth looks at him as she might a recently opened jigsaw puzzle splashed across the tabletop before her.

You're such a baby. You're such a little baby. You want to know something?

She generates a sound very close to a hiss and turns toward the door.

This is totally stupid, she announces. I'm going back.

She turns toward the door and something in Friedrich turns, too. He knows she knows what he knows he is going to do in another second and her knowing makes him feel ashamed, yet he is already asking her to stay because it is not something he can help. Lisbeth stops, hand on the rusty knob, considering. Friedrich hears himself promising he'll be good. He'll do anything she wants.

The bee is back at the windowpane, ticking, and the horse-drawn cart has moved on, and the past continues humming to

itself distractedly as it glides through hushed rooms between Friedrich's ears.

Lisbeth's thumb and forefinger slide down to the latch.

The tumbler clacks locked.

And the moment enlarges, becomes glassy with reality, every
corner of the shed taking on glistening highlights.

Okay, she says at last with a sigh, fine, fine, fine, Fritz, except it isn't
Lisbeth's voice speaking to him anymore.

It is Cosima's.

Surprised, he raises his head to find himself strolling arm in
arm with her along a sugary snow-packed path lined with gray-
green pines on the southern shore of Lake Lucerne.

It is Tribschen. It is 1872. The Franco-Prussian War is behind them and Friedrich's first book has just appeared. Wagner has
read it and there is nothing as unspoiled as the appearance of one's
first book. All the other books one will ever write will in some sense
amount to the same book, the same sensation, diluted, but one's
first is all about a glowing promise. Anything can happen immediately before and immediately after one's first book's publication.

Cosima and Friedrich are arm in arm in bulky winter coats,
deeply engaged in discussing nothing special. She points out the
appealing shape of a leafless larch on the hillside up by the villa
and Friedrich speculates on the species of a small bluebrown bird
hopping atop the snowcrust.

It is a perfect winter day.

Friedrich feels relaxed, loose.

He takes in a lungful of frosty air and holds it.

Four or five meters ahead, Wagner isn't so much strolling as
plowing through the afternoon in his Dutch painter's costume with
his gnarled walking stick, shouting observations about *The Birth of
Tragedy* over his shoulder in great clouds of steam.

Snow powder dissolves off the dipping branch of a pine. The atmosphere micas. Richard calls back: *Astounding, Fritz! Astounding! You are the only real benefit apart from my dear Cosima that life has brought me! You have arrived, my friend! You have arrived!* Cosima and Friedrich laugh. Cosima calls out *Everyone loves you, Richard!* and then squeezes Friedrich's arm like they are sharing a secret.

Friedrich met them four years ago in Brockhaus, shortly after Cosima left a mediocre pianist for Wagner. Friedrich assumed he had been invited to a musical soirée that evening and dreaded it, but when he showed up on the doorstep in an old suit in the middle of a downpour (he had had a new one made especially for the occasion, but at the last moment discovered he couldn't afford to pay the tailor) he discovered it was to be a private meeting instead. He couldn't believe his luck. The master and his mistress wanted to talk to the clever young philologist about Schopenhauer, and the clever young philologist couldn't hear enough about the master's theories concerning Total Artwork, the aesthetic chimera that would fuse and confuse music and drama and painting and mime. They hit it off brilliantly, exchanged ideas until past eleven, and, by the time Friedrich said goodbye, a genuine friendship had opened up between them.

A few weeks later, Friedrich began what would become regular visits to continue their ongoing conversation. They took daily walks, spent evenings listening to Wagner play the piano, shared round-robin readings of Hoffmann's fictions by the fire. Mornings, Friedrich worked on his university lectures and brought to fruition his monograph on Wagner's renaissance of the Dionysian in art before descending the twenty steps from the second floor into companionship.

As his mother and sister fell farther and farther behind him on the tracks, unable to keep up, Friedrich came to think of Richard and Cosima as his adopted family, the one that would usher him into this new period in his life.

Anything can happen immediately before and immediately after one's first book's appearance...and then the possibilities begin to close off, drop away. Friedrich wanted to deliver a centaur into the world by producing philosophical music with words rather than notes. Under the cloak of scholarship, he wanted to lure his readers out onto the dance floor and break up their thoughts by thinking. But truth was no one said much of anything about *The Birth of Tragedy* after its publication. Slowly a few reviews bobbed up here and there which were universally negative. They argued Friedrich had broken ranks with serious philologists, adopted a facile intellectual dilettantism, made an unsightly joke out of Greek culture.

Friedrich hated the academic factory for how it hobbled across the town square instead of waltzing. It was the age of the railroad and vaccinations, of blast furnaces and fertilizers, of the founding of the German Empire and the creation of the postal system, and yet scholars turtled their way along doing what they had always done in the manner they had always done it because they could not bring themselves to conceive there might be something else to do in some other mode. They were unable to wish for more. It was a terrible thought to contemplate: how an immense number of mediocre minds were occupied with remarkably influential matters. Anyone stupid enough to follow rules deserves them.

And yet here he is.

Here he is on this perfect winter day, arm in arm with Cosima, listening to the most eminent artist of the nineteenth century inflate his head with praise.

Richard already applauded *The Birth of Tragedy* in public, and, when Friedrich contemplated resigning his professorship to take up work as a publicist for him in Bayreuth, Richard dissuaded him on the grounds that Friedrich still had a few things left to teach Basel.

What is important is Friedrich feels truly healthy, truly satisfied, only when he has just produced something. The weather on those days is always invigorating. What is important, what would always be important, is this stroll, this afternoon, the way the sun astonishes the snow along this tree-lined path stretching out before them.

Think of it, Fritz! Wagner is shouting back over his shoulder in clouds of steam, plowing forward into the alpine splendor. *Think of it! What a sense of pride knowing I need no longer provide commentary on my work! I can leave everything to you! I am in capable hands! I am in the hands of an exceptional young talent who understands precisely how the great Wagner liberated art by shitting with Dionysus on the mythological stage of world history!*

Listen to what I am about to say!

It is the most profound thought Wagner has ever had!

Are you listening? Because Wagner says: fuck l'art pour l'art! Fuck the petty symbolists! Stand back, he says, and behold Herr Professor Nietzsche, behold the genius of the primordial mystery!

Except Friedrich is not in the snow anymore. He is in the attic. Wagner is gone. Ariadne is gone. The Sirens have fallen silent. An hour ago, surely no more than two, he entered an extended passageway. The surface of the wall along which he ran his right hand for steerage was abrasive and porous like coal. He tried counting his footsteps to keep track of his progress in the dark, only he lost the tally somewhere around two thousand. He shuffled forward so long he began to suspect perhaps he wasn't shuffling forward at all. Perhaps he had come to a halt and was puppet marching in place, hand resting on the wall for support, energy all burned up.

No, he is sure he was moving: hot air passed over him, his hand kept tracking along the gritty plane, convinced sooner or later it would locate the genitalia of a door. It was simply a matter of time. Anyone who knows how to listen well to music knows the most poignant thing about any composition is how it will always eventually end.

Then the passageway evaporated. His hand was tracing coal. His hand was tracing air. Friedrich developed two theories to account for this. First, there was a chance the passageway had opened onto a colossal room, a blackout hall, whose borders Friedrich could no longer detect because they were so far away from him. Second, there was a chance Friedrich had never really been in a passageway at all, but rather had fancied it because the human is the only animal to experience boredom, and hence there is art.

He pauses, breathing, sensing heat emanating from his body. The best thing for a person in life, he decides, wondering which way to go, which way he came from, what exactly he is doing here, where here is, what time of day it is, what month it is, what century it is, when he will find his bed again, why Ariadne has departed and left him like this, which is heavier, lead or longing, why his mustache continues to grow when everything else about him seems intent on shrinking, is never to have been born.

He reaches down to loosen his belt buckle and free some of the tightness around his distended belly.

Then he remembers he isn't wearing a belt.

Then he remembers he isn't wearing trousers.

Then he remembers his belly should no longer be distended.

He has taken care of his watery business: of this he is one hundred percent not unconfident. Yet his belly feels like there is a baby kicking inside.

He decides the second best thing for a person in life is to die as soon as possible.

At which point he hears a door slam.

A door?

A door.

Startled, Friedrich flinches and the baby inside him flinches and Friedrich's hands flap up in search of safety.

It is Richard, and Richard is furious.

Friedrich and Cosima are sitting very quietly at right angles to each other in plush chairs in the gaudy drawing room at the family villa in Bayreuth. They are listening to Wagner rage upstairs. He is slamming one door, tramping across their heads, slamming another, tramping back, opening and re-slamming the first.

Friedrich's chair is so soft and so massive he worries it is trying to consume him. His elbows are up around his ears. He is sinking fast, and Cosima is asking him how he could do such a thing.

How could you do such a thing, Fritz? she is asking. What were you thinking? What in heaven's name were you thinking?

Friedrich, sinking, glares straight ahead, refusing to answer.

It is Wahnfried. It is 1874. In January, Friedrich's second *Untimely Meditation* appeared, and almost no one except a few polite friends took notice. In February, he looked up from his lecture notes to discover he was teaching a total of five students. In June, Brahms gave two concerts in Basel. Friedrich attended both. Afterward, he bought the large red bound piano score of *Triumphlied*. Packing for his summer visit to the Wagners two months later, he tossed the score into his suitcase on a whim.

Not a whim, strictly.

It was no secret how much Richard disliked Brahms. He found him fatuous and restrained in a manner only a good German pretending he wasn't fatuous and restrained could achieve.

Friedrich didn't think much better of the music, but that wasn't the point when he left the score on Wagner's piano his first night at the villa, so that every time Wagner entered the room he would see it and know who brought it. Before going to bed, Cosima slipped it into the piano bench. The next morning Friedrich woke early and put it back on Wagner's piano.

Brahms had forgotten Dionysus, but that wasn't the point when Friedrich made sure he was playing his music as Cosima and Richard returned from their stroll through Bayreuth's city center that afternoon.

Friedrich had excused himself from the constitutional, saying he needed to stay behind to get a little writing done, and then paced the villa until he heard the couple returning up the walk. He trotted over to the piano, took his seat, and launched into the composition fortissimo. Bent over the keyboard, Friedrich could hear the heavy front door open and close. He could hear Cosima and Richard's laughter break off. He could hear Richard blunder up the staircase as if without warning he had become a bull.

Now Friedrich is being ingested by a large plush chair while Cosima is asking him what in heaven's name he was thinking. Richard rumbles and cracks above them. The summer air is warm and dead. The drawing room reeks of Richard's too-sweet patchouli. Glaring straight ahead, Friedrich thinks about what Friedrich was thinking. Friedrich was thinking that Richard was a fraud. That is what Friedrich was thinking. Yet he cannot bring himself to articulate this idea fully because he cannot find it within himself to hurt Cosima.

This isn't hurt.

This isn't even close to hurt.

True, Richard continues to talk and write passionately about musical revolution. Watch him in public, though, watch him interact with the self-important bourgeoisie and frilly aristocrats, and you don't see a redemptive artistic tempest. You see an overdressed sycophant prancing back and forth, relishing the attention he is receiving. Attend one of his performances, and you don't see the beginning of tomorrow. You see overbearing people more interested in a good meal and a good bottle of wine than in being made new.

Lately, the Total Artwork has seemed to Friedrich less about absolute transformation than about amusement and entertainment at any cost, a banal spectacle designed to keep the herd distracted, eager to return for more.

Listen closely, and you can hear angel wings flapping lightly among its notes, and Friedrich hates angels.

Talk to me, Fritz, Cosima is saying. We have been good friends for…how long? How many good times have we shared? Richard has worked diligently on your behalf. He has helped your name gain the circulation it deserves. How in the world could you bring that…that *composer* into our house by way of thanks?

Friedrich wants to be angrier than he is, but he is unable to rise to the occasion. There is a moment in most friendships when the friendship inexplicably becomes something less than itself. There is a hole-in-the-heart curve you round where the collective history and agreeable feelings dematerialize with the minor recognition of the way someone lifts a glass of brandy or scratches his neck, although no one involved can bring himself to acknowledge the modulation.

Wagner was funny and outlandish and brilliant and faithful. Now he is just one more of Friedrich's illnesses. Friedrich understands he will not be returning to Wahnfried, will not be returning to Tribschen, will not be meeting with the Wagners for another year, maybe two, and then only as someone else.

With that, his ego becomes a figure of speech and his face starts to soften.

Friedrich looks fatigued on the field of thought.

Step by step, he blinks himself back into this drawing room and back into this warm too-sweet summer day. He sits up in the ominous chair, turns to Cosima, reaches forward, and lays a graceful hand on one of hers, smiling awkwardly.

They remain like that.

I'm sorry, Ariadne, he says at last. I really am. I don't know what came over me. Sometimes I'm not myself and then I am. I'm sorry. Do you think perhaps we could go upstairs together to apologize?

Okay, she says with a sigh, fine, fine, fine, Fritz, except it isn't Cosima's voice speaking to him.

It is his llama's. It is Lisbeth's.

She tests the latch on the tool shed door and next she is standing in front of him in her Easter dress, less impatiently, the furry bee back at the windowpane.

You have to do everything I tell you, she says.

Friedrich nods.

Because this thing? You think it's going to be one way, only it's something else completely. Look...

And then she is showing him with her coarse hands some of the many methods by which a human being can be punished because slaves need masters as much as masters need slaves, and this is how we purchase clemency, and this is how we purchase forgiveness.

Tell me what I am doing, she says, doing things.

What?

Tell me what I am doing. Say it out loud.

Friedrich, kneeling beside himself kneeling, begins to narrate the present moment expanding around them and expanding through them and he feels at home and he feels farther away from home than he has ever felt.

Tell me what I am doing now, Lisbeth says, and he does. He tells her and tells her. The telling makes him feel slack and alert at the same time.

And now, she says, her pewter eyes shut and sandblond pigtails

dangling down behind her, Easter dress white with pale blue cornflowers. Tell me what I am doing now.

Friedrich kneels beside himself kneeling on the packed dirt
floor, sweating, powerfully aware of the mud-spattered shovel,
the rake, the trowel hanging on rusty hooks, the rusty bucket and
rusty watering can on the dilapidated gray table in the corner, the
dust circulating in the day's growing heat, the ancient scent of soil
and the bright scent of his sister, trying for a while to remember
what it was he was meaning to remember, and then giving himself
over fully to the joyful shameful remoteness of this event, because
thoughts are to the brain as bile is to the liver.

And now, says Lisbeth. What now?

You are doing this, he says softly, making his sister vocabu-
lary.

And now?

You are doing this, and I am doing this, and you are doing this, and now you are doing this, and now this, and this, and
this…

9 p.m.

I believe…

What do I believe?

I'm not sure, actually.

I believe…

I believe…

Give it a second.

Give it a second.

I believe someone is reading to me.

Yes, that's it: someone is finally reading to me and evening is a slow gray seep and my visitors have departed, taking their expenditures with them.

I am at that point in the course of a visit when I am sure no one will ever visit me again. Somehow I had expected more. And someone is finally reading to me from...

I want to say someone is reading to me from one of my favorite novels...

Unfortunately, I have temporarily misplaced the name of the novel's author.

The name of the novel's author and the name of the novel.

The name of the novel's author, the name of the novel, and the name of the characters frequenting it.

Despite such apparent setbacks, I recall with great clarity that the scene at hand represents the turn in the narrative where let us call them C and D, who once were together, are no longer so. Having traveled immense distances side by side, having gathered many remarkable adventures along the way, they have become separated. Events have transpired. Some were more interesting than others. Then more things happened, from what I can remember, and here they are.

On the water.

On a river.

They are on the river in a fog and, while once together, they are now apart.

C, for want of a better name, is riding the raft, D the canoe.

All I need to do is keep my chin up for a few minutes longer and then they'll let me go to sleep.

We thereby have yet more proof, should anyone require it at this late stage in the argument, of let us call him Y's comic genius. It is no exaggeration to suggest he knows more about water and inclement weather than almost any writer who ever lived. The story about the American Odysseus who found Ithaca insufferable: I once offered to send a copy to Overbeck.

Overbeck or Burckhardt.

Either of whom politely turned my offer down.

Something, perhaps, was lost in the translation.

Something always is.

But the high drama, the youthful spark, the fog knowledge: what more could one ask from a serious work of literature?

I want to say...

I want to say it is my mother who is reading to me.

Yes: my eyes aren't what they used to be, this much is beyond debate, and yet I recognize her love voice.

When she is finished, they will leave me alone.

It all comes down to passing a little more time.

I believe...

I believe...

There. I've done it. Another few seconds over the shoulder.

I remember as a child lying beside her, my mother, listening to her read, the white afternoon light another fog I was buoyed up in.

Every day, before my nap, after Lisbeth had been tucked in for hers, my mother entered my bedroom bleached with sunlight and, in a ritual we enacted until I left for school, I carefully un-dressed and took my position beneath the covers, sheet tucked to my nose, staring earnestly at the screen of my imagination, while she, propped on several pillows beside me, recited.

Other books by other authors with other characters, to be sure, and none of which I can bring to mind at the moment with anything resembling clarity, but I remember with immense preci-sion the lying there.

My thoughts running, me buoying there beside her in the pond of particulate brightness, making up things in my head.

The good times.

I believe they call such instants *the good times*.

I can think of none better.

It wasn't the stuff of the stories. That wasn't the important part. The important part was the resonance of my mother's love voice telling me that history always happens in the future, that all this will be more consequential in half a century than it is today, yet this afternoon, Lisbeth sleeping in the room nearby, we will read together like this, just before my nap, just before I drift off on the liquid rhythms of her recitation.

C and D...E and F...U and V: I remember them well, whoever they are, were, once together and now apart.

On the river in the fog Q hears R's whoop and paddles toward it, except, as he approaches the spot from which he supposes said whoop issued, it activates again, this time not in front of him, but to the right, and so he changes course.

Another whoop expresses itself, which may or may not have issued from the same whooper, not to the right but behind him.

Then another, not behind him, but to the left.

A question of Boolean logic, in the long run: if W is neither in front of X, nor behind him, nor to either side, is it clear that X has lost his father as I have lost mine?

My mother reading.

The story unfolding.

My imagination hurrying forward.

This at a stage in my life when our maid stopped my mother in the kitchen one morning to worry aloud, as I ate my breakfast, about the poor near-sighted boy who was so idle she witnessed him sitting in the drawing room staring into space for hours on end.

But what is this I feel on my fingertips, rubbing them together, trying to rub them together?

I raise my hand to perform an inspection.

I try to raise my hand to perform an inspection.

But my hand is not my hand in the dimension that lives closer to us than our own skin.

My hand is the head of a black snake, its graypink mouth gaping.

My bed is full of them, black squirmings, some no thicker than a piece of string, some massive as a length of plumbing pipe, and there is a vocal perturbation in the atmosphere, quite possibly my own...yes, I am almost certain the vocal perturbation is mine, mine and then my mother's, she running her hand through my hair and saying *there there, there there*, because we can never see or touch the things that really matter, can we, and so I look up.

bowels

You look up from your lecture notes to discover you are teaching a total of not five but three students all of them incompetent and your bowels loosen slightly at this understanding. It occurs to you for some people consciousness is a dangerous tenement whose rooms they should never enter alone. With each book you publish each lecture you deliver fewer and fewer show up to hear you and those who do occupy the precise balance of oxygen and nitrogen in your classroom with unreadable postures and unreadable expressions waiting for you to make a fool of yourself drop your papers lose the bread crumb trail of your argument do something preposterous. You can see it behind their unreadable eyes but you

have no alternative other than to press on into the scholarly abyss
and so you say *Good morning* in a quiet voice on this first day of
your series of talks on the Pre-Socratic philosophers addressing the
clock on the back wall thin snowflakes hanging in the air outside
the windows the wide green Rhine beyond the bridges wooden
ferries like Chinese water taxis and having no alternative other
than to press on you say into the vacuum of their features *I am
Herr Professor Nietzsche and I will be your labyrinth. My task this semester
is to make you uncomfortable.* You are being watched by three people
who display a profound shortage of emotion the classroom blustery with soundlessness aside from the processing of your bowels
never your friends and your audience waits to see what you will do
next because they need the credits and what you do next is look
down at your notes and look up again and you realize thinking is
a form of peristalsis and some people are born to be animate ob-
structions so you skip the rest of your introductory comments and
drive straightaway into your thesis. *I should like to begin by putting forth
the observation that the first difficulty with the problem of morality is that no
one realizes it is a problem. This is Socrates's fault. The rest of the history of
philosophy from Plato through today has therefore been at base a crisis in mne-
monics.* You catch the open countenance of the youth in the third
row and appreciate you are engaged in many activities at present
but none could accurately be described as teaching. You remark
the way his mouth is busy not closing and interrupt your comments in mid-thought to ask *Does anyone perhaps have a question at this
layover in my lecture?* But the youth's mouth remains busy not closing
and the student two rows behind the first student is content taking notes or perhaps catching up on his correspondence while the
student in the back corner appears to be reading an important text
printed on the ceiling in ink invisible to everyone but himself. You
appreciate education in these people's minds is a form of defective
entertainment you might as well end the semester by passing out

questionnaires asking them to rate your performance so you leap over the examples that shape the meat of your talk and enter the paragraph housing your conclusion why not. *It thereby follows, in a manner of speaking, that human morality evolved from the morality of animals, please don't hesitate to interrupt me if you sense a question coming on, which is to say we believe because our hairy ancestors believed what harms us is evil while what profits us is good, I would be only too happy to clarify any of these assertions for you, needless to say, all you have to do is fire me off a flare, and hence, you see, what Socrates misplaced is the affirmation that morality is obedience to the truth of biology, not the truth of spirit, this will be on the exam, and thus morality is obedience to custom, and it therefore stands to reason in German culture's glorification of work one sees the expression of fear of the individual, an entity that strikes terror into the heart of every barnyard creature, and if you disagree with me I urge you to please raise your hand, that's all you need do, the forces of musculature and gravity are designed exactly for such exigencies, and we can discuss these notions like adults, and so the questions I would like each of you to ask yourself as our semester together advances are simple, straightforward, and triadic in nature. First, why do I live? Second, what lesson have I to learn from life? And, third, why do I suffer from being what I am? Which leads me, unless anyone might have another perspective to proffer concerning these matters…which leads me to urge each and every one of you, by the time your examination presents itself, to become who you are; neither agree nor disagree with me, but grow; know that the identity theorem which states A equals A applies only to the sphere of logic, that there is nothing truly identical with itself because there is nothing that remains the same even for the moment of comparison; and therefore to live in the happy astonishment of finding yourself dancing in the perpetual flames that structure terra infirma…. Class dismissed. Thank you. Go away.* It takes almost a full minute of hush to prod the youth in row three to consult his watch furtively and another full minute for him to realize your introductory lecture has occupied slightly fewer than eight minutes and another full minute for him to hoist himself sideways in his seat and consult his fellow youths exchange whispers less furtively consult his watch again and softly seemingly politely gather together his materials rise collect with his colleagues at the back like a small family of anxious meerkats to file as much as three mammals can give rise to such a metaphor out the door blessed are the sleepy for they shall soon drop off. Your warmest smile accompanies them and when the classroom is resonantly vacant you flip back to the beginning of your notes cough demurely into your fist and begin again from the beginning to deliver your lecture to the one audience member who can honestly appreciate the stunning luxury of its fury and fight.

raids of an untimely man

Let us see what the day has to offer, Friedrich announces to no one, stepping out of his tent onto the remains of the battlefield and pausing at the threshold.

He scans the smoking devastation under a gray summer sky.

Turns.

Reenters his tent, thinking better of his plan, and zips closed the flap.

Eyes shut, he sits erect on the edge of his cot, wondering what the point of vision is, precisely, if this is an example of it.

It is Wörth. It is 1870. In July, Bismarck made public a telegram from Kaiser Wilhelm altered to appear insulting to the

French. A few days later, France, although wholly unprepared, declared war. Friedrich applied for leave from his teaching duties at Basel to make himself useful as a nursing orderly with the Prussian troops. A week later he is here, poised to push toward Paris behind the advancing Southern Army.

His part in this campaign, he recites, his only part, standing again, laying a soiled hand atop his head to hold down his body, could not be more simple: help gather the corpses and the wounded and bring them to the designated area where they can either be buried or tended. And it is time to get going, he recites, taking his position on the cot once more.

It is time to get going, except.

He shuts his eyes and palms his sore kneecaps.

Except what entered his lungs yesterday, still a good kilometer away from this place, took on the character of grilled meat with a seasoning of spent gunpowder. A fecality dyed the breeze. Friedrich could taste the reek at the back of his mouth.

Then his supply convoy crested a small rise and saw what had been until earlier that day the front lines. Outnumbered and outflanked, the French employed chassepots and mitrailleuses to hold off the advancing forces for eight hours. When they began to retreat, they had lost one-third of their men.

Everything was ashen, smoldering, at odd angles, cockeyed, crisscrossed, as if a folktale dragon had swept the battlefield with its colossal tail before spraying it with fire. Friedrich cut down into the damage with a group of orderlies. Twenty meters on, he tripped over a large charred tree limb half-submerged in a clump of scorched grass and landed on his knees. Hard. His comrades hoisted him up and patted down his outfit. Preparing to strike off again, Friedrich noticed the others looking behind him at the cause of his fall. Friedrich looked, too, and saw the large charred tree limb wasn't a large charred tree limb. It was a large charred torso, the head and legs of which had entered the realm of irrational numbers.

He excused himself and withdrew behind a stand of burned lindens where he attended to his unfriendly bowels.

When his comrades' laughter strayed into the distance, he reappeared, and occupied the rest of his day wandering a torched pasture that appeared to be growing bodies and body parts, listening for the music of groans.

He remembers very little of it.

He is thankful for that.

What he does remember, though, sitting erect on the edge of his cot, rubbing his sore kneecaps and trying to swallow away the aroma smearing the inside of his mouth, is the single arm he discovered lying next to an overturned cart.

It belonged, he could tell from the uniform, to a Frenchman.

Its fingers were still crossed.

Friedrich crouched, picked the thing up by the rubbery thumb, and, exerting more pressure than he had anticipated, broke the inflexible digits to reflect the cosmos.

For most philosophers, he decides, eyes shut, wondering how long it will take someone to find him hiding in here like this—for most philosophers, philosophy is nothing in the end besides a longing to reach home.

The peculiarity is that he is both already there and still nowhere near.

It is just like Odysseus, only without the hope of Penelope, and every daytime a nighttime.

The current state of affairs has been going on for what Friedrich would guess has been twenty years. He has made no progress whatsoever. His spine is a broken broom, his feet grand pianos, his mind a bowl of melting ice cream. There is nothing to do save lie down.

Good.

He has said it.

There is nothing to do except lie down in this infinite attic and sleep. Perhaps tomorrow Telemachus will find his bed empty and mount a search.

Friedrich stalls in the amnesia of light, gathering strength for the multifaceted task of lowering himself onto the floor he believes should exist somewhere beneath him. He recognizes the process has commenced when he hears components comprising him pop and crack. He is reminded of the noises the maid produced in his mother's kitchen when disassembling the carcass of a chicken on the counter.

At length, he finds himself lying on his side on the wooden slats, head cradled in elbow crook, knees fetaled up to his cranky pregnancy. He remains there, listening to air displace air in his nasal passages. It sounds like a fierce Atlantic wind.

And next he is in his bed at 18 Weingarten, sheets tucked up to his nose. It is a staggeringly bright afternoon. His mother is propped among pillows beside him. She is reading, although he cannot make out the particulars of the story. Her words are muffled and slow, spoken through a tubful of water.

Why did you do it, Fritz? she is saying soothingly. Why did you leave your post at the University? We all felt you could do anything. But now look at you: almost forty-five, unmarried, and I am still sending you socks and sausages. What happened to you? What did you do with my son?

He blinks and a white cup of weak green tea sits before him on an outdoor café table.

With his pinkie, Friedrich examines a chip in the saucer.

He has for now forgotten where he is. This is not a problem. Of late, it happens a little almost every day. He decides to let time and place steady and slides his glance across the red and white tablecloth and up, and, yes, there she is: Lou opposite him, her own teacup hovering a centimeter from her lips, eyes expectant.

Friedrich tries to recall the question she just asked him, while chewing on the idea that his head is inside the head of another person, and that that head is in turn inside still other heads: everyone is someone else and no one is himself.

His eyes stray above and behind her, taking in the bay windows of the baroque Apelshaus. This is, he wants to say, Leipzig. They have, he wants to say, been strolling. That's it. They have been spending the afternoon visiting Nikolaikirche and the Royal Palace. It is teatime. Rée and Frau Salomé have peeled off to find Bach's tomb under the apse in Thomaskirche. Friedrich and Lou are alone for half an hour. In a week, he will wake up beneath the sofa in his hotel room to find all three gone, friendship and love outmoded concepts.

Still, this moment is the present one, the one that makes all the difference, and it is late afternoon and the sky looks like rain and the air is damply cool.

No, no, he answers, all at once recalling where he is in the conversation. I simply wasn't getting enough real work done. My schedule was demoralizing. Every weekday morning I delivered a lecture at seven. On Mondays I held my seminar. On Tuesdays and Fridays I taught at the gymnasium twice, on Wednesdays and Thursdays once. Every evening, as I closed my office door behind me, on my way home to outline more classes and grade more exercises, I asked myself what I had accomplished that day, what I had done that I would still be capable of bringing to mind in six months, and, well...

Lou touches the cup to her lips and sips.

A blackbird scuds across the nippy grayness above the marketplace.

Silverware tinkles around them.

Someone else raises her voice to say *I don't believe you!*

Friedrich feels more comfortable with Lou than he has ever felt with anyone in his life. He feels uncluttered, satisfied. He watches with pride as she reaches down by her feet and lifts her handbag into her lap, clicks it open, extracts a slender cigar and silver box of matches.

Other patrons steal disapproving glances as she lights up.

Lou is clearly aware of them and gains a great deal of pleasure from their displeasure, so Friedrich gains a great deal of pleasure from it as well.

She leans back, crosses her right leg over her left knee, and relishes the first three puffs. Then she begins coughing. She lurches forward, hacking into a handkerchief. Friedrich believes he can make out a pinkish stain in the white bouquet.

Are you all right? he asks.

My lungs are in a bad mood today. I think they're pouting. I should think you would have been a wonderful teacher. You *are* a wonderful teacher. I can just picture you in front of the classroom in your suit. Do you want to split a sweet? The tortes look wonderful.

Thank you. No. He examines the chip in his saucer. I suppose the question is how long one still feels the need to collect acolytes. The impulse seemed increasingly like a character flaw.

You should put more into your stomach in a day than green tea, you know.

Friedrich feels more comfortable with Lou than he has ever felt with anyone, yet his bowels are not his friends. They never have been. For years he ate no flesh in an attempt to effect an armistice with them. Wagner convinced him such an undertaking was ludicrously contrary to Friedrich's nature. Vegetarianism, Richard told him, is a mode of living for those bovine individuals who aspire to be nothing more than digestive machines. Intellectually productive temperaments need blood like wolves and Weimaraners. Friedrich ate nothing else for months until his guts ground to a halt.

He currently bears in mind the asceticism of great men and ingests cleansing green tea throughout the day, a small portion of fish or fowl and rice for supper, water in the evening. The status of his digestion has not improved. If anything, it has worsened. He cannot understand what he could be doing wrong.

An almond croissant, then? Lou persists.

I don't believe so… Yourself?

She is back at her cigar, which she is holding between her thumb and third finger as if it were a chocolate bonbon she were about to pop into her mouth.

One evening this past summer on holiday in Tautenburg, she entered his room without him hearing (he had left the door open for the fragrant twilight breeze) and stepped up behind him while he stood at his window watching the last glow of sun and put her arms around him and said over his shoulder *This is perfect, isn't it?* They had spent the day walking the narrow goat paths lacing the hills, talking about so many things it was hard to keep them all straight. There had been a moist grassy smell and a sense of growth everywhere. Friedrich watched the sun lessen, enjoying Lou's violet perfume. He thought about how in one sense it *was* perfect, and how in another they had already failed at something, and the saddest thing was being there to watch Lou pretending hour by hour that they had not failed.

I don't believe I can pass up one of those tortes, she says. They seem like just the thing this afternoon. I am positive I have been secretly dreaming about them for days.

Order one this minute, says Friedrich. Indulge yourself.

Lou's face cheers.

You're right. You're absolutely right. Somewhere in this café exists a torte on which my current happiness depends.

Lou appreciates her cigar. Unexpectedly glum, Friedrich fingers the chip in his saucer, trying to tease out a metaphor. He feels the presentness of the present receding. A veiny-cheeked waiter in a black vest, white shirt, and black trousers sets the torte in the middle of the table. He has brought two forks. Friedrich reaches over and hands one back. Lou stubs out the cigar in her saucer and admires the richness of the sweet's paper-thin layers.

On the first day of each semester, Friedrich says as she picks tiny pieces away from the corpus of the cake and lays them on her tongue, closes her mouth around them, closes her eyes, savors—on the first day of each semester, your students approach you with empty hands. Your job is to fill them with what you already own. You watch them running the obstacle course, which from their perspective is an always-novel undertaking, while you stand on the sidelines behind your podium, coaching them to sprint faster, a little slower and thicker yourself every day. It was just a matter of time before I began to cultivate the professor's obligatory hump and stupor.

Systems and vampires, Lou says with a mouth full of crumbs and cream filling. Neither can see themselves in mirrors, while both take all you have to offer and insinuate you haven't given enough. But ask either for something in return, and the indignant silence is palpable…

She swallows.

She pursues the bite with a sip of tea.

Fingering the chip in his saucer with his pinkie, it occurs to Friedrich it is no problem having thoughts. The problem is getting rid of them.

The veiny-cheeked waiter returns with the bill.

Friedrich waits politely for Lou to pay it.

His bowels are not feeling well at all. He holds his breath, releases it, rises, walks around the table, and stiffly helps Lou with her chair, surreptitiously locating his cramping guts with his palm.

He is in the Karlsruhe hospital lobby, panting, panting and sweating, even though it is a mild September morning and he has not exerted himself in the least. He would consult with the sky about his options, but it feels as if someone has just slipped a knife into his side. He keeps his eyes directed earthward, observing his shoes, noticing they could use the slightest bit of polish.

In Ars-sur-Moselle, his company took charge of a large group of casualties and detoured back toward Germany with them. For three days and three nights he and a comrade named Mosengel, an awkward doughy man several years younger than Friedrich, nursed six bad cases in the back of a cattle truck as it clanked and brattled across the countryside. Four men had shattered bones and could not stop themselves from screaming whenever the truck encountered a bump. Gangrene had taken hold in the two others.

Less than half an hour ago Friedrich, Mosengel, and several soldiers delivered their charges to the hospital.

Descending from the third floor to the second on his way to a nearby café and a cream cake, the blade went in. Friedrich recoiled. His hand flew out in search of the banister.

He bent there, immobile, waiting for the end of the world.

In another life, he might have been a philosopher. He loved to think and loved to argue and loved the nervous heat when his mind was sharp and engaged with an interesting problem. He knew he would be capable of original ideas if only he had time to clear his head of his students' voices and his mother's and his sister's. Then he would be able to hear his own. He was certain it would bring him considerable news.

Only somehow the inertia of his education had carried him

into a professorship, the war had carried him onto this staircase. He was already in his mid-twenties and he had produced nothing worthy of a second glance. He had done what was expected of him. He had risked nothing.

If he survived his present predicament, he would edge into middle-class middle-age with a few good lectures about the ideas of others beneath his belt.

This was a nightmare.

A minute later, the blade slid out and Friedrich was standing upright again, wondering what all the fuss was about. Health rushed back into him. He loitered there, catching his breath, laughing to himself, and soon resumed his descent, attributing this spell to bad food and the press of the war.

Stepping into the lobby, a second blade went in.

In the space between footfalls, Friedrich became a bowing maître d'.

The membrane lining his throat seared. The nerves branching down his arms became scrambling cockroaches. With great effort, he raised himself erect and shuffled ten more paces toward the main entrance, aware people were starting to take notice.

Someone is standing beside him, asking him something, but Friedrich cannot hear him because a high-pitched whine is stuffing the alcoves of his brain. The sound is the color of sunlight splashed across the limestone blocks comprising the Syracuse amphitheater.

He hates to draw attention to himself in public. All Friedrich really needs to do is walk outside, inhale some fresh air, acquire a glimpse of the sky, and he will be fine. But his elephant feet will not budge. Someone smelling sweetly of chloroform is standing very close to him, asking him something, touching his arm and asking him something again, and then someone is gripping his left elbow, and then someone is gripping his right, and then his bowels become a burning rage.

A surge of hot blood and mucus spills down his legs.

Sentient life is an enormous error, Friedrich concludes, going under.

Back to the peace of sand.

Back to the silence of stones.

10 p.m.

Dysentery, they said.

They said dysentery, inflamed belly mad with parasites, and carried me back upstairs.

When I awoke, I was occupying one of the beds next to one of the beds occupied by one of the soldiers I had just delivered.

Then they said diphtheria.

Dysentery and diphtheria.

You need not feel you have to choose, apparently.

There was the swollen throat. There was the assortment of toxins boiling in my veins. There were the diverse offensives against my heart and nervous system and the immense colorless desert called insomnia stretching out ahead of me every night.

The only thing more terrible than falling into an endless uneasy sleep, ground giving way beneath you, is not falling at all.

The inability to lose Flying Robert's flying mind.

The inability to close your eyes for more than thirty seconds before feeling the urgent need to open them again even though you know there's nothing of particular interest to see out there.

You cannot think fully.

You cannot feel fully.

You thinkfeel feelthinking your way through the laboratory your body has become.

And so.

And so.

And so you tell yourself stories to make the darkness move.

Once upon a time, you tell yourself, Schopenhauer was visiting a greenhouse in Dresden. He became so absorbed in the contemplation of one of the plants there that he began talking to himself out loud about it. This drew the attention of an attendant, who approached warily and asked: *Who are you?*

Schopenhauer looked up from the plant, startled.

He searched the attendant's face intensely and replied: *If you could only answer that question for me, I'd be eternally grateful.*

I usually lie here and shed tears and scream and grow young. I am being watched. It feels not wholly unpleasant. I should perform the great extravagance in order to determine who is speaking, but I am tempted to say my eye-opening days are behind me.

No dear, says the expenditure. You rest.

Sometimes I am fairly confident I am still alive because I can still produce an idea.

I have to keep living because I have to keep feelthinking.

I recall returning to Basel at the end of October that year, after the dysentery, after the diphtheria. I was never quite myself again. But then, who is?

And now I am being tucked in by hands other than my own hands. Pillows are being adjusted around me. Perhaps it is my mother running her fingers through my hair.

I want to say it is my mother.

I want to say it very much.

A few more minutes, and people will leave me alone. First the bedpan. Then the behavior water.

Once upon a time, you tell yourself, Goethe's mother lay on her deathbed. There was a knock upon the door and the servant girl entered with an invitation to a party. The old woman listened to her, reflected, then mouthed an almost inaudible reply, which the servant girl painstakingly recorded on a piece of elegant stationery.

Frau Goethe, it said, *is regretfully unable to attend your festivity. She is busy dying at the moment.*

I became young very late in life.

In my old age, it took fifty grams of chloral hydrate a month to knock me out and put behind me my headfires, swollen eyes, stomach knots, fevers, constipation, hemorrhoids, chills, sweats, waking exhaustion, pulsing joints, treadmill thoughts.

In my current youth, I am no longer so easily swayed by the odd opiate.

They have less effect on me than a brief massage.

Perhaps I have thought this before.

Perhaps I have not.

Once upon a time, as I say, Hegel lay on his deathbed. He wavered in and out of consciousness. After a long period of silence, he gathered his strength and whispered: *Only one man ever understood me...* He remained quiet several minutes, then added: *And even he didn't understand me...*

After all, the greatest events in life happen not during the loudest hours, but during the stillest.

Not during the most crowded, but during the most solitary.

This is why cattle can never be quiet.

The light is out. The curtains are pulled. The commotion withdrawing.

It has been a busy day.

The tumbler clacking locked.

Footsteps on the stairs unhurriedly turning into recollection gaps.

And so.

And so...that's it, really.

That's all.

The harmonious era of nothing entering the present tense.

The real fun just beginning.

hands

You observe your right hand composing in lamplight your left curled like a small hairless animal on the desktop and you realize you told yourself you would work for only an hour after dinner but already it has been four. You ate alone down the street in the Sils-Maria hotel restaurant because you always eat alone there because a peripatetic hammer philosophy is a little more like the grave every day. You took your table at the back of the dining room considered every item on the menu the tea sometimes too strong the food too spicy even the water known to disagree with you. The hazards are innumerable and so you ingest no wine no beer no spirits no coffee no cigarettes no cigars no sugar. You exchanged as little conversation with the waiter and your dining neighbors as possible because these days hearing your own voice alarms you. You ordered a piece of broiled whitefish unadorned with sauce and a side order of plain rice a single slice of plain bread sans butter a cup of green tea and you passed time listening to conversations taking place around you resigned that not one of these people had any idea who you were. Those in the greater world who do know who you are wish they did not. They hold you in lower regard than your most casual acquaintances. You have long ceased to be concerned with friendship even Burckhardt has become your father confessor. Twenty-six years your senior the blue-eyed historian with the close-clipped white hair has made his aim the meticulous enumeration of your sins under the guise of amity keeping watch for small openings in the conversation during which to reintroduce your resignation from the university your latest foibles missteps misdemeanors indiscretions social peccadilloes scholarly heresies logical contradictions in avuncular cadences that in their self-effacing self-righteousness evince his unmistakable hunger for control. While Burckhardt has started to confuse sleepiness with wisdom Overbeck has dismissed each of your new books with a few kind words in concise notes proving he failed to read even the first paragraph. Squat Malwida believes every word you have ever written is an excuse to talk about squat Malwida and her continual fear that not enough people love squat Malwida as whole-heartedly as squat Malwida might wish. You have long ceased to be concerned with friends because you are concerned with your work and after your meal you rose crossed the dining room courteously thanked the waiter returned to your *chambre garnie* on the second floor of the flax-colored house with the green shutters backing against the mountainside at the edge of town telling yourself you would write for one hour although when you consulted your watch just now you realized it had already been four and it is past midnight. Flimsy snow flakes down outside even though it is July and notebooks manuscripts proofs open monographs are piled around you on your desktop and across the floor and your one possession a heavy wooden traveling trunk containing your two shirts and spare suit is propped in a corner its lid ajar and on your bedside table sits a tray crammed with medical bottles. There is not one flower or framed photograph in sight no decorations your room heated by the cheap stove your mother sent you that produces more noxious fumes than warmth. You prefer working in a chill because it makes you feel awake but this is too much by half and so you are wearing your overcoat your woolen scarf your fingers having a difficult time of it you have on your double glasses your nose hovering eight centimeters away from the desktop. If you squint you can just make out your thoughtinsects advancing down the page. You finished part one of *Zarathustra* in ten days in January slept from one a.m. until four and you are nearly finished with part two convinced your current work has become epochal opera. Of course no one notices of course that doesn't really matter of course that does. Of course you are not writing for them of course you are of course you are really writing for the few who someday will notice of course you will be dead by then. Of course something bad is happening to you you cannot tell what it is you would rather not think about it. You do not speak much these days because you do not like the sound of your own voice but when you do speak your speech sounds faintly slurred like people who have had small strokes. You forget things you have always forgotten things but these days you are forgetting things you never used to forget and sometimes you forget what those things are and all you can recall is that you have just forgotten something. You will stop in the middle of the lane by the rushing brook remembering you have forgotten why you are on this particular lane at this particular moment and your headaches can no longer accurately be referred to as headaches they have attained a new category of being. You stop writing lay a hand on top of your head read the lines you have just written: *Forgive me my sadness. Evening has come; forgive me that evening has come.* You cannot recall whether you have already written something similar elsewhere (and if so have you written it better or not as well?) or whether you have just invented it. You take your hand off the top of your head pick up your pen prepare to push forward because you are sure you still have a good thirty forty minutes left in you before something falters and it is time to stop for the night *there is an isle of tombs the silent isle there too are the tombs of my youth* how strange someday you will forget having composed that line you will forget sitting here like this writing here like this thinking about forgetting what you will have long ago already forgotten.

my impossible ones

Friedrich uses his mind to cross his cold sunny flat, leak through the door, and crawl behind his bony landlady's bony face as she ascends the stairs, cleaning bucket and mop in hand.

When he turns around inside her, he is peering through a pink-skin mask with filaments of copper hair frizzing at the margins of his vision.

The first thing he comes to understand about Signora Fino is that she does not so much think about the world as exist pervaded by it. She experiences how the late-morning winter light overwhelms this stairwell, how thumb-sized clouds of dust are continually maturing wherever two planes converge to form an angle. The second thing he comes to understand is that from her perspective Professor Nitzky is not so much an individual as a detail consisting of further details. He is his considerable whiskbroom mustache and a pair of straight-razor eyes.

It is Turin. It is 1888. It is two days after Christmas.

At present, Signora Fino is being pervaded by curiosity about her lodger. Professor Nitzky is almost blind, always reserved, especially polite. He pays his rent on time and, whenever the opportunity arises, mentions his descent from Balto-Slavic nobility with satisfaction. I speak in German, he has told her on more than one occasion, but I feel in Polish.

Sometimes she bumps into him wandering the bright landing above the enclosed courtyard, slightly stooped, talking to himself, his woman's hands echoing his thoughts. The instant he sees her, he cuts their strings and his severe expression softens into an eager smile and greeting.

Very good, she says, and yourself?

Oh, dying, he responds, but otherwise fine.

No sooner does she round the next corner than she hears his words set off again on their own private path behind her.

She can never fathom what he is going on about.

This, she supposes, is the nature of professors. Signora Fino has heard all about what goes on at universities—a big fuss about things you cannot touch, a great damming up of human potential. She supposes it's good work if you can get it.

Professor Nitzky winters here and does not teach. How can he call himself a teacher if he does not teach? No one visits him. He receives few deliveries. He disappears for walks lasting hours every day only to return and lock himself inside his room for hours more.

This is not the problem. Every lodger should leave such a small footprint in Signora Fino's wakefulness. The problem is that neither Signora Fino nor her husband has seen Professor Nitzky since the day before Christmas Eve. He has not ventured out of his flat. No guests have joined him for the holidays. He has attended no church services. Earlier this morning, when she pressed her ear to his door, Signora Fino heard nothing, not even that special concentration of atmosphere signaling another human being's presence.

This worries her.

She moves pervaded by an awareness of dust clouds, curiosity, and worry.

Because, two years ago, there was that other lodger, that fat Englishman who breathed like a bellows with a leak. He was a professor, too. When he spoke to her in the stairwell, Signora Fino could not help imagining his torn lungs fluttering inside his chest cavity.

He vanished behind his door for nearly a week before she and her husband took notice. Eventually they went up to his room and knocked. Nobody answered. They let themselves in with the master key. The fat Englishman was sitting in a wooden chair by the window, head angled back in amazement, mouth doing a silent aria. His fat arms hung like fat sausages at his fat flanks. The pill-bottle cork he had choked on was still visible at the back of his fat black throat.

Signora Fino and her husband did not like people dying in their boarding house.

The other lodgers nattered.

Business fell off.

And then Signora Fino had to touch the same furniture death had touched and death inevitably left an oily residue that infected her with the recollections of strangers.

This morning, after she pressed her ear to Professor Nitzky's door and heard nothing, she went straightaway to her husband's newsstand on the corner across from the cab stand and told Signor Fino everything. Signor Fino listened, picking at the patchy reddish beard on his dried-fruit neck, and, when Signora Fino concluded, told her to get her mop and cleaning bucket and go upstairs and have a look through the keyhole.

The fat Englishman had had little boys up to his room. Thirteen- or fourteen-year-old little boys. It was disgusting. It gave Signora Fino thoughts. But the Finos were the first to admit the fat Englishman did not make a racket with his puppies. He was admirably discreet. He paid his rent on time.

Live and let live, Signor and Signora Fino said.

Then the double-gutted pillow biter went and choked himself to death.

Pervaded by an awareness of dust clouds, curiosity, and worry, Signora Fino steps onto the landing and stops to catch her breath in the late-morning winter light.

She lowers her cleaning bucket and mop. Straightening, she becomes conscious of the peculiar clumping in Professor Nitzky's room. Signora Fino awoke in possession of sore feet, unpaid bills, too many rooms, a bad back, and too much airborne dirt. Now it sounds like someone is rearranging the furniture in there. Rearranging the furniture is strictly prohibited. Allow a lodger to move one piece, and pretty soon he asks to move another. Allow him to move another, and pretty soon there are conflagrations in the Piazza Carlo Alberto.

Signora Fino consults the landing for stray tenants and, seeing none, assumes what she is sure is a slightly unladylike crouch at the keyhole.

She inclines toward the mechanical orifice and closes her left eye and applies her right to the undertaking and has a quick once-over. Midway through, her bony hand flies up to her mouth. On the other side of the door exists a different order of things:

Professor Nitzky is performing a dance. He waltzes gracelessly with himself, leaps onto the bed and drops into a simian stoop, bounds back onto the floor in an elegant, what do you call it, pirouette, each turn covering nearly half the free space in his flat. He is winded and wheezing and his eyes are squeezed shut and his skin is splotchy scarlet and he is naked.

Professor Nitzky is naked and his man things are bobbing.

His shoes, socks, shirt, tie, and suit lie scattered across the floor and draped from the small armoire in the corner. He scoops up his underwear and places them atop his head like that hat the lodger back from South America wore, a, what do you call it, a Bolivian chullo. Then Professor Nitzky disappears.

Puzzled, hand continuing to muzzle her mouth, Signora Fino leans forward, right eye rolling in its socket, searching.

Everything in the flat has gone black as ignorance.

Signora Fino presses forward and readjusts her posture, yet it is as if she were looking down a well at midnight. It takes several seconds for her to understand Professor Nitzky is kneeling directly on the opposite side of the door, maybe six centimeters away from her face, peering back at her, sending his galaxy through the keyhole into hers.

He is speaking under his breath between wheezes. His low muffled voice seems like it is originating behind Signora Fino's wide-open eyes. *Good morning, Donna Fino*, it is saying. *Have you by any chance seen the sky today? It is a glorious blue more blue than the color blue itself and there will therefore be no mistakes in here, I am happy to inform you they are impossible now, you can tell these things, and so we should consider such a day lost if we have not danced at least once, should we not? Would it therefore perhaps be too presumptuous of me to ask if you might care to join me for a quick turn? I should regard your company as the greatest of honors. Come, let me undo the lock... Let me undo the lock and then a quick salute to Terpsichore and then back to work for us both. I shall show you how my eyebrows*

have been growing. Such is my sister's surprising strength. What do you say?
Cut loose. Cut loose. Let a god dance through you...

A noise somewhere between a blat and a chirp emanates from the other side of the door, then the cleaning bucket clatters onto its side and a series of heavy footfalls thumpity-thumps down the stairs.

Friedrich presses his eye closer to the keyhole and discovers he is not looking at the landing in his boarding house in Turin, but at the northern Italian countryside scudding past in a browngreen smudge. Lou is not resting her head on her mother's shoulder, Frau Salomé not surveying the landscape from beneath her feathered hat, Rée not reading a Swiss newspaper.

In their places, small-eared Overbeck is watching Friedrich with very tired eyes, his face puffy, chalky, his lower lip pouched as if sucking a thumb of chewing tobacco. Beside him sits a young bespectacled man with an ostrich neck. His arms seem to sprout from his spinal column the way chicken wings do.

Overbeck, watching Friedrich, smiles wearily.

Friedrich smiles back.

The young bespectacled man smiles because everyone else is smiling.

Friedrich cannot seem to recall what the purpose of such lower facial manipulations is, yet he feels sure one should always match like with like.

Smiling, Friedrich looks out the window.

The growing Alps form the teeth-horizon that marks the frame of the world. Beyond are krakens and mothers. Friedrich feels uncomfortable and then he has a question.

Trying to formulate it, something else strikes him: Friedrich is smiling because smiling is what you do in the presence of friends. Friends are people who help each other. Overbeck helped

Friedrich by reading Friedrich's books for almost twenty years even when Overbeck did not really read them, and he helped Friedrich by knocking on Friedrich's door when nobody else would knock on it.

Friedrich let him in, crossed the room to the upright piano in the corner, and demonstrated specifically why his music is clairvoyant.

He explained while playing how sometimes he was Friedrich and sometimes he was a man named Hanswurst and in either case he consulted the egg fissured with blood vessels growing on the ceiling, big as a football and wetly amphibious.

With every chord, a new version of the future pumped inside it.

That is where Friedrich first saw Rée climb over the railing and leap to his death from the bridge he and Lou used to stand on when courting.

That is where Friedrich saw a bald woman named Imogen, no, Ingrid, no, Ilka, no Imogen, walking down a burned-out street in Dresden, dragging what was left of her skin behind her. Wisps of smoke curled off her back and charred legs like spirits.

You could not see the egg at the moment, needless to say. Friedrich explained this to the keyboard, which in turn explained it to Overbeck. Eggs were frightened of the heads of critical theology departments and memories of their considerate wives and evenings they all spent together talking university gossip and petty politics.

As Friedrich made this last point, the young bespectacled man with the ostrich neck appeared in the doorway of his flat. Overbeck introduced him as Herr Miescher. Herr Miescher told Friedrich about the important man in Basel wanting very much to meet him. They needed to get a good night's rest, Overbeck added, so they could catch the first train in the morning. The important man (a prince or a publisher, Friedrich can't recall which) would meet with the philosopher only if the philosopher behaved himself on the journey. Would Friedrich do that? Would Friedrich behave himself?

Friedrich would.

Friedrich did.

And here Friedrich is, hurrying toward the ragged frame of the world, everyone smiling because that is what friends do with their lower faces when in proximity to each another.

Friedrich concentrates on sitting still, sitting erect, sitting like a proper professor. His feet want to move. He fights the urge. He raises his hand like a good student and waits to be called on.

Herr Miescher exchanges looks with Overbeck. Overbeck nods at Friedrich and says:

Herr Nietzsche?

Friedrich rises and thinks thoroughly about his question before asking it. If it is a prince, he is about to be knighted. If it is a publisher, he is about to be read. This is no time for foul-ups.

I can no longer seem to lose myself, he announces with abundant politeness. Could one of you gentlemen...could one of you gentlemen perhaps see your way clear to help me?

Of course, Herr Nietzsche, Overbeck responds, worn.

Overbeck and Miescher exchange further looks, then the latter shifts in his seat, reaches into the pocket of his jacket, and extracts the vial of chloral.

Thank you, Friedrich says. Thank you very much.

He takes his seat, smiling, waiting patiently to become someone else.

Out the window all the trees lining the dirt road have turned into human arms. Hands are riding bicycles through shady flickerings. Hands in wide-brimmed straw hats are cutting through the pastures.

Above the rolling browngreen landscape, smaller hands circle in the clear winter sky.

Hunting.

The very important man in Basel was named Wille. He was no taller than a filing cabinet, wore a pair of oval pince-nez attached to his lapel with a gold chain, and thought so noisily Friedrich could hear him even when he did not make use of his mouth. With great composure, Friedrich shook his hand and answered a number of interesting and less interesting questions. During the first lull in the conversation, he asked deferentially if Wille were a prince or a publisher.

A prince, Wille said without hesitation.

Would you then perhaps care to sing the gondola song with me? asked Friedrich. I am quite exhausted from my journey and am tempted to say we titled Poles think along the same lines.

Possibly later, Herr Professor Nietzsche, replied Wille. I'm afraid we have a few things we ought to attend to first. Would you care to accompany me? I should quite like to show you the rest of my palace.

Friedrich turned to Overbeck and Miescher, who were standing just inside the door of Wille's office, and winked.

Would you two gentlemen care to accompany us? he asked them. I'm sure His Excellency would be nearly as delighted as I at such a prospect.

In a plain room on the second floor, they asked Friedrich to put on an attractive white robe and presented him with a tiny beaker of royal liquor. They helped him into bed, telling him he should try to sleep a little before the evening's banquet, then took their leave. Although fatigued from the trip, Friedrich could not seem to bring himself to lie flat on the mattress. Flat or on his left side or on his right. After much investigative shifting, he found the most agreeable posture could be attained by sitting back on his heels in the far corner.

His mother arrived two days later. She wept with pride when he explained to her how the high courts of Europe had after all these years finally discovered the undetermined animal called Friedrich Nietzsche. Had he not promised her someday to prove he had been worth her trouble?

The next afternoon his procession continued to Jena to meet the esteemed Otto Binswanger who, rumor had it, was in control of delicious cherries. Friedrich ate his fill and fell asleep for several months until, one day, the intensity of the four suns shining through his window woke him up. He hunkered in his corner observing them corkscrew through the afternoon sky. Then he saw they were not outside his window: they glided, dipped, and spiraled above him in his room like fist-sized fireflies, long slender manta ray tails trailing behind them. Friedrich reached up to touch one of the light sperms. Initially, its language sounded like static, then like thousands of tiny children trying to speak in unison.

The earth has a skin, it said. The skin has diseases. Please say goodbye to your species for us. It was stupid, lazy, and selfish, but it had a magnificent sense of architecture.

When Friedrich regained his senses, he could remember nothing that had happened since last November except that special visit. He was no longer entirely sure where he was. But what mattered was his sheets were clean and he felt refreshed and breezy-headed. His mind was sparking, his body prickly.

Friedrich climbed out of bed in fine humor, crossed the room, and parted the curtains. Above the terra-cotta fishscale roofs, an ambient gold scintillation tinged the whiteblue sky. If he had to guess, he would say it was morning. If he had to guess, he would say it was spring. If he had to guess, he would say he was standing in his mother's house in the tidy room on the second floor in which he grew up.

A walk, therefore, was definitely in order. First he had to dress himself and locate his notebook and pencil. Then he would set out on a vigorous ramble to celebrate the flawless day. He seemed to remember his mother telling him to remember something sometime earlier.

Give it a second.

Give it a second.

Wait for her.

Yes, that's it: wait for her to accompany him to the market.

First dress, then find his notebook and pencil, then wait for his mother by the front door, and out they would go to delight in the atmospherics.

From behind the mask that is Overbeck's face, the world looks washed-out.

Melancholy clings to table legs.

Brightness is an infection.

The man lying in bed before him is the most negligible object he has ever seen.

It is Naumburg. It is 1895. It is late September and, as Overbeck stands there at the foot of the bed in the room in which his old friend grew up, Friedrich feels the thought enter him that this will be Overbeck's last visit.

Overbeck is queasy with guilt. He experiences what an act of betrayal feels like from the point of view of the betrayer, yet he knows he does not own the fortitude to attempt another one of these horrid things. He looks at Nietzsche lying there, semi-conscious, flinching involuntarily, and tries to imagine none of what has actually happened has actually happened.

Perhaps his friend has suffered a minor accident. Perhaps

he has taken a fall. Perhaps he will be up and about in no time. Only a year ago, after all, Overbeck had been able to stroll with him through the streets for hours. Nietzsche knew him and knew himself. They had conversed at length about books, beliefs, mutual friends. Then one spring afternoon Nietzsche stopped in mid-sentence in mid-street, suddenly unsure where he was, and Overbeck saw in his friend's panicky eyes that there was no swimming back for him. The waves were too high, the riptide hungry.

I should like to go home now, Nietzsche said. My concepts are spilling. I should like to take this opportunity to apologize in advance for what some of me are going to do.

Alwine said he hardly slept anymore. Because of his nocturnal restlessness, he spent his days exhausted in bed. Sometimes, when she was cleaning downstairs, she heard him abruptly raging above her, cursing, pounding the walls. By the time she hurried upstairs and threw open his door, he had already tucked himself back into bed and was staring apathetically at the ceiling, struggling to stay awake.

Late in life, Overbeck thinks, standing at the foot of Nietzsche's bed, you often hold on to your friends even when you can barely endure them. This is so there will be someone there to regret your passing. Hold on to them as tenaciously as you like, but your friends will eventually drop away. Some will die before you die. Some will almost undetectably slip out of touch with you and disappear from your life, until one day it occurs to you with a mild shock they are gone and have been for years. Some will deliberately break their ties with you or you with them because as you get older it is very nearly impossible not to begin hating other people for what they are and what they do and what they do not do and what they are not.

Overbeck pictures himself gently shaking Nietzsche into awareness, and tries to formulate some parting words with which he might leave his friend. Something about how much he, Overbeck, always desired a relatively ordinary life, about how he would never have had it any other way, one placidly predictable day after another, one dinner party, one new book, one dissertation defense, one stroll with his wife, one lecture on the familiar material, and yet how a part of him has always envied, even admired, Nietzsche for turning away from all that on a street corner over a decade and a half ago, and simply walking away.

Overbeck lets time incandesce around him.

He lets the room hover in pale colorless light.

And then he crosses to the door and steps out.

Are you perhaps my mother? Friedrich asks the woman he finds cradling his head in her lap.

I am, precious, says the woman. Are you awake now?

Unable to move his head, Friedrich employs his peripheral vision to take in his surroundings.

Are we perhaps home? he asks.

We're in your room. Outside is a beautiful autumn evening. You can smell the leaves through the open window. Can you tell your mother your address?

He concentrates.

It is always the same one, he says after a while.

We're so proud of you, she says. Do you know why?

I believe I once knew the answer to this, but I cannot seem to recall it at present with any exactness.

We thought you had lost our dear God forever, but you have found Him again, haven't you? Do you remember what you said this morning when I told you our friend Eva had passed on in the night?

Friedrich lies still, killing time.

You said: *Blessed are those who die in the Lord.* Do you remember?

He tries to shake his head no.

Well, it doesn't matter. The point is you've made your mother very happy. Somewhere, your father is smiling down at you. Can you see him? You should hear your sister. She goes on and on.

Friedrich senses disturbance. Next his mother's weight is bowing down. He senses the light puff of air created by her upper body descending. He senses the dry kiss she bestows on his brain through his skull.

It feels precisely like a scalpel.

third part:
on the vision & the riddle

11 p.m.

I learned when I was seven...seven or eight...the particular year escapes me...I learned when I was a boy, at any rate, that it is easy enough inhabiting the heart of a paragraph.

In the heart of a paragraph, you know your longitude and latitude.

You know which way the want is blowing.

Then *scarlet fever*, they said.

One day they said scarlet fever and, for the next fortnight, Johannes de Silentio lay among fever dreams, sunburn rashes, and a torn throat, learning that inhabiting the transitions is by far the more difficult state of affairs.

Inhabiting the transitions, I learned as a boy of seven or eight, is when you begin hearing Nero tuning up behind the torched curtains. All the cream cakes are gone. The only noise left is the sound of your own breathing.

The gale. The cave.

The cave. The gale.

Between paragraphs, there is nobody with whom to think about the future of humanity.

Conceivably this is why people produce children. Somebody to help you use up the minutes. Somebody with whom to wait for the tram.

I did my children the favor of never having them.

When I began my recovery, my mother and aunts carried me out to the veranda. They wrapped me in a dark plaid blanket and tucked me into a chair among the rampant flora where I could view my sister playing in the garden below among dabs cotton-balling spring trees.

Occasionally, on the nearby lane, a dapper man in a bowler hat pedaled past on his thick black bicycle. I wanted to accompany him wherever he happened to be going. I had the impression I was always a day short of where I was supposed to be.

My llama tells me we are not in Naumburg anymore. She tells me she built me a new veranda here. The maid wheels me onto it daily to air me out. There are, she tells me, photographs. I know nothing about it.

I lie among these sheets, listening to her, sweating and thinking, sweating and endeavoring to think, knowing that between paragraphs home is where the hurt is.

On rare occasions I have felt in some small degree less lonely than I do at present.

And so, once upon a time, I tell myself, one of his students happened across Diogenes talking to a statue of Athena in the middle of a busy street in Sinope. The student approached the great cynic, waited for a lull in his one-sided exchange, then asked respectfully the reason for such pointless conduct.

Quiet, please, Diogenes replied without turning away from the marble of his desire. *I am busy exercising the art of being rejected.*

That is to say: I suppose things could always be somewhat less fine than they are at this particular moment. Too much dampness in the air or not enough. Much warmer. Much colder.

Because...

Because...

Because we compromise ourselves by going in a straight line and meaning...

I've lost the road, I'm afraid.

I had it, but then I lost it.

A certain chronological arrhythmia settling.

And so.

And so.

And so...*Ma chère luminosité,* I write (in my head: I write it in my head), because writing exaggerates your personality the same way sex exaggerates your personality—by making you exactly who you are.

Ma chère luminosité—

I have begun to be quite unprecedentedly famous. I thought you might find some minimal amusement in this. From what I can recall, no mortal has ever received such letters as I, and only from the most exclusive intelligences.

Let us say simply: St. Petersburg.

You should hear the tone, and please come collect me.

The concept-albinos at Basel have put Oedipus through the mercury cure in an attempt to immortalize him. The vapor baths. These are not celebrations in the ordinary sense of the word.

The Wagnerites have applied moist heat using pieces of white woolen flannel, while the Christians have resorted to the detestable mechanics of the Revulsive Sitz Bath—which is to say they gain Odysseus's favor by allowing him to lounge in the warm mineral springs, and then, as he rises for the towel they hold out to him, they throw a pail of cold water upon his privates.

(Death, of course, being a mere prejudice.)

Most Affectionate Greetings,
Your Old Creature

Carissima—

It has been five full five seconds since last I wrote you and still no reply? I fear the worst. Doctors everywhere, their taste in shoes nothing short of contemptible.

From now on it is every well-dressed man for himself.

I swear to you I would send directions if I possessed them, but, as it stands, you must trust your instincts.

Strike forth.

Knowledge chokes.

Forever Yours,
Hanswurst

My Muteness—

My greatest mistake in life, it now occurs to me, lying here in the dark heat, is that I have imagined the sufferings of others as far larger than they in actual fact are. The most debilitating danger for me will always lie in my capacity for pity.

(Whatever one brings into solitude grows.)

Or, to put it more plainly, children are the gifts that rob you. Zarathustra knows them as Excuses for Why I Fail in Life: I cannot take a trip because

I am busy raising my piglets; I cannot write because I am busy suckling my litter.

This is the answer to the riddle of why I have accomplished next to nothing: my groin called, and I answered.

And to these people I say, O my dearest hush: He who cannot learn to fly higher should learn to fall faster.

My point being, as always...

Being...

My point being...

What?

nervous system

But in the current version you do not drown because in infinity there are just so many stories so many worlds and then they begin repeating themselves and when you try to lift your arms in the glacial water you find yourself swimming. Your rowboat bobs and thwacks on the choppy surface three meters away eight meters two the white wooden bulk presenting a growing threat as you close in. It is strenuous work your muscles frosted shreds of steak and you slip back under sputter awake start all over again. But at last you heave yourself in thumping onto the boat's floor curled into yourself shivering lightning at the bridge of your nose piloting you to the black brink of consciousness. With the back of your soggy sleeve you wipe at the snot the blood streaming through your mustache cough and that's when you become aware of someone else sharing the rowboat with you. A remote attentiveness at first you too exhausted to move your head then you hear bodyweight shifting. You look up and see a little blond boy sitting erect above you and see the little blond boy is you. He is wearing black cuffed shorts oiled hair parted down the middle he is seven eight looking back at you. His face is carmine-and-cream his steamy spectacles thick a cartoon personification of a bookworm. You ask him what's the matter he reaches up and with the back of his sleeve wipes at the mucus seeping out of him and says shyly *How did your mustache get so long?* You laugh and laughing sit up push back your clingy soppy hair rub your forehead with your thumb and third finger and when you raise your head again you say *That's what you came all this way to ask me?* The younger you examines the older you reckoning your tone snorts up a great gob with an abrupt nasal in-suck. *Why?* he begins and stops. *Why what?* you ask. *Why did you become who you are?* You look away the fog in which your boat sways phosphorescing in the moonlight like your nervous system. *Because* you say looking back *because you won't have any other choice. You'll think you do, but ultimately it will just seem that way, only, it's not so bad, is it?* He examines you and says *You'll never get married* and you ask *Do you know what friends are?* and he shakes his head *no* water lapping the evening smelling darkpinegreen. *They are the people who know all about you and decide to like you anyway. You're going to have plenty of them. You'll gradually outwear each, like your sweaters, but that's okay too. It's just who we are.* He says *Sometimes my stomach hurts* and you say *In a few weeks you're going to meet two boys, Pinder and Krug. They'll keep you company at school. Pinder's father will read you a story by a man named Goethe and you'll fall in love with language. Krug's father will play you a piano sonata by a man named Liszt and you'll learn why music makes life bearable and you won't be lonely after that, not really, anyway* and the boy raises his head quickly as if hearing a far-away voice and you say *You're listening to mother. Can you tell what she's reading?* He says *Flying Robert. She's gotten to the part where he's disappearing into the sky. He ought to have listened to his parents, oughtn't he, and never gone outside in the first place on such a windy day.* You reach forward pat him on the knee and say *It's a story Fritz, but do you want to know something, even mummy doesn't know about it?* and he says *What?* and you say *Flying Robert is enjoying himself up there, he is really loving it* and the young you removes his spectacles wipes his swollen eyes puts them on again. *It's been quite nice* he says and you say *Before you go, would you do something for me?* and he says *I'll try* and you say *That's good. Love yourself, Fritz, you've got to learn to love yourself like mad, do you hear me?*

i want, once & for all,
not to know many things

Friedrich presses his left eye closer to the keyhole and discovers he is not looking at Signora Fino on the landing of his boarding house in Turin, but at his sister and that idiot Förster in Förster's room at the hotel in the Naumburg town square.

Lisbeth is standing in front of him in her hollygreen Christmas dress.

Förster is kneeling before her, reddish-blond beard jutting out from his lower face like a hairy shovel blade.

Lisbeth's dress is up around her waist.

Watching, Friedrich is appalled by how untidy Förster's hotel room is. How untidy, and how Förster is divested of clothes save for his exceptionally well-polished boots, which Friedrich admires to a far greater extent than makes him entirely comfortable. Förster possesses a thin, unmuscular body and a fist-sized swell of flab above each hip. His skin is the faintly jaundiced color of Brie.

It is December. It is 1882. It is a holiday. It is cold in this hallway and snowy in the town square and Friedrich hates holidays. He grudgingly trained up from Rapallo for this one, and will return the moment it is over. Every year, as Christmas encroaches, loneliness spreads through him like a barbiturate. His family comes to seem bearable in his mind's eye, then necessary, and finally he experiences a tenderness toward them, a longing for their company, that makes him feel like a failure and a hypocrite. An hour after arriving, he is planning his escape.

This time they gave him a small oil painting of the Virgin. He bought his mother a beautiful black shawl, his sister a boar-bristle brush, Förster a fine pearl-handled knife from Switzerland. They gave him socks and a small oil painting of the Virgin.

Look at this, he said, opening it.

Friedrich didn't mean the declaration to sound like an accusation. He attempted to convey in his voice the enthusiasm he assumed they wanted to hear. Rising from his seat on the living room couch, he dutifully kissed his sister on the cheek. He gave his mother an automaton embrace. He shook hands stiffly with Förster, who afterward raised his glass of apple cider in a toast to the evening. Friedrich glowered at the candles burning among the bushy branches of the Christmas tree and set about devising his exit.

Franziska, imagining him in high spirits, asked if he might like to accompany the trio to mass in the morning.

Friedrich said he didn't think so, excused himself, retired to his room, and tried very hard to fall asleep.

Now the air in this cold hallway is sour with coal smoke and Parisian perfume. A brash man's voice exclaims something on the landing above him. Another man answers. Heavy footsteps clump through the inside of Friedrich's head. Someone could descend the staircase behind him any second, or perhaps open a door along the corridor, or a bellboy round the corner and happen upon him like this. Friedrich knows how ridiculous he would look. The great German philosopher who has written next to nothing crouching in his heavy darkgray overcoat and darkgray scarf and black gloves like a natty bullfrog on the plum carpet before the white door, left eye pressed to the keyhole.

How, in the course of his life, did he arrive here?

At one time, there seemed to have been so many other places to go.

He appreciates the fact that he should push back this instant. He should stand and turn and walk away. He should catch a cab to the train station, a train back to Rapallo, and never set foot in this town again. Lisbeth is thirty-six, Förster thirty-nine, his mother nearly fifty-seven. Friedrich is thirty-eight and he should push back this instant, yet he cannot—not after he has followed his sister through the light snow collecting like dust bunnies along the streets. Not after he has seen what he is seeing. He is appalled by how untidy Förster's hotel room is. Most of the bedding is scattered across the parquet floor. A pair of smart black trousers is bunched on the table amid a used blue-on-white Meissen tea set. Undergarments are prevalent. A single teaspoon sparkles in the middle of the bare mattress.

After Christmas Eve dinner, Förster took his leave with a series of overdone bows. Half an hour later, Franziska excused herself and went up to bed. Fifteen minutes more, and Friedrich heard his sister slip out of the house. He threw on his coat, scarf, gloves, and followed.

He finds it inconceivable one would conspire to make a bad impression on a maid. Every morning, when he hears the cleaning woman's cart creaking up the hallway of the pension where he is staying, he quickly rises from his writing desk and fluffs his pillows and makes his bed, combs his hair and trims his mustache, puts away his toiletries and latches his trunk. By the time the cart halts outside his door, he is ready to receive his visitor for the day.

Because the overman's existence is built upon the sacrifice of the underman, except.

Except.

Except one mustn't merely have the courage of one's convictions. One must have the courage to question them.

Otherwise, the point of thinking is…what, precisely?

Give him ten minutes. Give him twenty, and this room would stand in unspoiled order. Fold the clothes. Slip them into the wardrobe. Remake the bed and turn it down for the night the way a bed ought to be turned down for the night. Put a chocolate lozenge, perhaps a rose, on each pillow.

Friedrich hears a noise behind him and spins around on his haunches, panic flishing in his weak eyes.

At the top of the staircase stands an immense form.

From Friedrich's perspective, there is something more bird-like about it than human.

It is Röcken. It is 1848. Barricades burn in Paris and Rome, Naples and Venice, Prague and Budapest, Vienna and Berlin.

It is Monday morning. In three weeks, Friedrich will turn five. He has been busy rolling a rubber ball in a slab of sunlight at the bottom of the staircase, mind empty as a winter flowerbox, until it occurs to him what he wants for his birthday. He wants a wooden rocking horse. Ernst down the road has a wooden rocking horse and Friedrich wants one, too. A wooden rocking horse with a painted-on smile and a painted-on saddle and a real mane made of real hair you can really pull. Hearing a noise above him, he scrambles to his feet, peers up: the immense bird at the top of the stairs resolves into an immense eagle resolves into his father.

Daddy, Friedrich announces with great conviction. Daddy, I should like a rocking horse for my birthday.

The Pastor stares down at him.

He wears swelling robes. His arms climb away from his sides like bat wings. He opens his mouth to secure the present, but his arms fold in around his face instead, and a shockwave passes through his body.

Daddy? Friedrich asks with somewhat less conviction.

The Pastor dullthuds down the staircase.

Then he is splayed at Friedrich's feet.

The slab of sunlight stretches, achieving a new variety of angles. Friedrich considers the thread of spittle sticking to his father's cheek. How The Pastor's eyes are slitted open, yet how the pewter irises are hiding beneath his forehead.

Friedrich begins to run.

Friedrich is running and Friedrich is shouting.

Friedrich is shouting and running down the hallway and out the back door into the orchard. He remembers his mother is hanging laundry there. His sister is sleeping in a crib in the shade beneath an apple tree.

The air peppy and cool.

Leaves glistering in the spiky light.

I did that! Friedrich is shouting as he runs, little hands over little head. *I did that! I did that! I did that!*

The first he heard about Bernhard Förster was as the crackpot teacher in a Berlin gymnasium who had organized a petition demanding the limitation of Jewish immigration, registration of all

Jews, and the exclusion of Jews from positions of authority in government and education.

Förster called the appeal *a cry of distress from the conscience of the German people.*

Friedrich called it a joke.

This is what happens, he told himself, when you throw the pack a bone.

Only soon nearly two hundred seventy thousand people across the country had signed the petition, and it wasn't funny anymore. Förster had become one of the leading figures in the anti-Semitic groundswell. By forcing him to resign his post, the gymnasium at which he worked simply helped make him into a national hero. Wagner heard his story, and promptly invited him to the Bayreuth Festival to see the first production of *Parsifal*. Lisbeth attended, met Förster at one of Richard's bashes, and fell head over heels for the dolt.

Worse, it was Friedrich who had insisted she go in the first place. He wanted to hear what Wagner was saying about him, and wanted a few weeks' peace in Naumburg so he could get some serious writing done before journeying to Tautenburg to rendezvous with Lou. He told Lisbeth the excursion would be good for her. She was, he told her, more than capable of taking care of herself.

Instead, she fell in love with Bernhard Förster.

How could she fall in love with Bernhard Förster?

She raved about him in letters to Friedrich through the autumn. With all the insight of a good German, his llama called her new beau an intelligent, honest, decent, hard-working, and forward-thinking man.

Friedrich wrote back saying anti-Semitism was a mutiny of the mediocre. People like Förster were motivated by envy, resentment, and fury in the face of their own intellectual inferiority. He was dangerous in that way only severely obtuse people can be dangerous.

Don't listen to him and remember to thank the Jews every day for giving you your God, the mightiest book in history, and the most effective moral code in the world.

Lisbeth wrote back saying Förster and she were getting engaged in January.

Friedrich wrote back saying she was no longer his sister.

But down in Rapallo, at the beginning of December, that awful loneliness commenced creeping through his nervous system, and before long he found himself looking at St. Wenzel's gothic dunce cap lift into view out the train window as it rolled into Naumburg.

Friedrich bought his mother a beautiful shawl and his sister a boar-bristle brush and Förster a fine knife from Switzerland. They gave him socks and a small oil painting of the Virgin.

It was portable, his mother told him, for easy transport.

Wouldn't it be nice, Friedrich reflected as he peeled away the pretty paper, to be able to trust one person in the universe, one person able to live up to his expectations of what a member of this species ought to be?

In place of that wish, he received the family surrounding him.

Look at this, he said, unwrapping, beaten down.

At dinner the night before, Förster had outlined his latest scheme over plates heaped with mashed potatoes, string beans, ham slices, bread. Friedrich ate only the potatoes. His digestive tract was not faring well. The instant his head stopped hurting a week ago, a sharp pain awoke in the slippery jumble of his guts. The doctor had prescribed cocaine for his flatulence, and told him to up the dosage after ten days if the initial measure didn't do the trick.

Friedrich picked at his potatoes while his brother-in-law to-be, mouth full of pinkish mush, explained how he would leave for Paraguay the following spring to conduct an extended investigation of German colonies in the Upper La Plata region. He planned to return within two years, at which time Lisbeth and he would marry. They would move to Paraguay together to build the New Germania, a utopian community where pure Germans with pure ideals could reinvent the country that grew a little less robust, a little more sullied, a little more dissolute every month.

Lisbeth and I will become, he announced with great solemnity, the new Adam and Maiden, and the New Germania a garden of hope in a jungle of despair.

Friedrich snorted.

A forkful of mashed potatoes became enmeshed in his mustache.

Förster carried on. He was already in negotiations with the Paraguayan government, which had agreed to lease a vast tract of land to him with the proviso it would become his property if he could introduce one hundred forty families within two years of signing a contract.

What could possibly be easier? he asked.

And what nobler? Franziska added from the other end of the table.

She adored Förster unabashedly.

Friedrich saw how her eyes gleamed with pride when Förster spoke. She looked at him the same way she used to look at Friedrich when he returned home from Pforta for the holidays and she sat in the living room reading the notes of praise scribbled by his teachers across the bottom of his essays, one after another, as though counting out large denominations of affection.

A bulb of methane dropped from just below Friedrich's right rib cage to his surprised sphincter and quietly liberated itself. If he were asked to choose a color to accompany it, he would opt for maroon. Maroon or perhaps red ocher with a trace of mauve in it. A shade, in any case, suggesting density, richness, and bite.

Lisbeth caught his eye and pointed to a buttery smudge on the left side of his nose he had missed.

Wiping, Friedrich watched his sister's beau's shiny lips move. He willed himself deaf. The pinkish mush in Förster's mouth reminded Friedrich of the Doberman he had seen yesterday morning arch its back at the foot of the fountain in the town square and choke up a clot of half-digested pulp it subsequently re-ate joyously.

Everything was consuming everything else.

Friedrich could barely bring himself to take another forkful.

All the filth of food.

The gristle.

The fat.

The blood.

Franziska's nose appears beneath the armpit of her polka-dotted blueblack dress as she pins a pair of work trousers to the clothesline strung between two trees in the orchard.

What is it, precious? she asks Friedrich. What's wrong?

Friedrich points back at the whitewashed house looming like two stories of apprehension above the trees.

I did that! he shouts at her. *I did that! I did that! I did that!*

Did what, precious? she asks, arms lowering unhurriedly.

That! I did that! That!

What, Fritz? What did you do? What is it, honey?

The augmentation in her voice: how gentle incomprehension modifies into escalating worry. How their eyes lock for a very long time that isn't really very long at all. Friedrich knows the laws guiding the physics of light have just changed, but his mother doesn't know this, but she will know it, but she doesn't know she will know.

How some things simply refuse to recede in memory.

His hands climbing above his head for safety.

And then he is off again, running, running yet not shouting, running and breathing, a gale rushing through the cave inside his head.

His route generates a wide arc around the side of the looming apprehension and takes him across the shrubby front farmyard, the man-sized wedge in the hedge, out among the willows gathering around the fishponds like billowing green filamentary clouds.

Everything touching everything, Friedrich understands as he runs, runs and breathes.

He squinches shut his eyes and is skimming through rosy emptiness. He pictures his mother crossing the patio, wiping her hands on her dress. He pictures her entering the hallway.

Everything touching everything.

Everything a luxuriant set of connections.

Leafage. Wickerwork. Abundance.

This, of course, is the problem.

This is the problem, and it always will be.

What is it, honey? Lisbeth asks. I can't hear a goddamn thing you're saying down there.

Förster mumbles something beneath her hollygreen Christmas dress.

She looks expressionlessly at the top of his head whose reddish-blond hair she has horded in her left fist and now yanks. Hard. Förster grunts, his leather boots creaking beneath him. With her right fist, Lisbeth endeavors to keep her underclothing free of her enterprise.

Bullfrogged at his post outside their door, it sounds to Friedrich as if Förster is mumbling a newspaper article from inside a wardrobe.

And now, Lisbeth is saying, pulling hard. Pulling hard and then pulling harder. What am I doing now?

Förster doesn't know how to play the game, Friedrich realizes, and so he picks up the slack: You are doing this, and he is doing that, and you are doing this, and now you are doing this, and now this. Friedrich slips his gloved hand between the flaps of his overcoat where the buttons of his trousers present him with several significant if not insurmountable hindrances. He is powerfully aware of the single teaspoon sparkling in the middle of the bare mattress. The four squeezed lemon slices on the blue-on-white saucer.

The way Lisbeth leisurely turns her head toward the door, knowing or perhaps only seeming to know.

The way her face registers or doesn't register his presence, then wavers back into vacancy.

Yes: that's it: *affection.*

This is what some people sometimes refer to when they say the word *affection.*

Friedrich is sure of it.

midnight

Almost sure.

Unless, needless to say, he is somewhat less than almost sure.

It is one way or it is the other.

Dreaming itself, you see, becoming an exhausting affair after a while. The body asserting itself. The colors flooding in. Your mind pacing back and forth across the stage, forgetting its lines one after another.

If, that is, you can call this *dreaming*.

Dreaming and not, say, something equally unsettling.

Being awake, for example, alive in the dark flames.

There's always that possibility.

There's always that possibility among others, because...

Because I think...

I think...

Not to put too fine a point on it, I think I smell rather musty among all this lingering and sweating, this sweating and endeavoring to linger.

Like one of my mother's old dresses.

I have become a variety of the various forms of passing.

Or...

Or the way, even as an adult, home for holiday, I sometimes snuck into my mother's room when she was elsewhere, stole over to her bed, and, still standing, lowered my face into her pillow, briefly, sniffing what a lifetime's failure of the imagination smelled like.

If it's going to come, let it come, I say.

Let it come.

This coming being the opposite of that appalling comedy Christianity makes of taking one's leave.

Except it doesn't come.

Nothing leaks into being.

I seem to find myself in a perpetual drizzle of about-to-happenness instead, skin after skin flaking away until there is just wind beneath these moist sheets, and then not quite even that, just this slightly distasteful afterscent.

I can feel myself departing the minds of others before I depart my own.

This is what it boils down to in the end, apparently.

It feels not unpleasant, I should perhaps take this opportunity to point out, not altogether unpleasant, like the odor of that stale pillow as I bent over my mother's bed, sniffing for something at once reassuring, cheerless, and inevitable.

Look: a few more seconds behind me.

That's the spirit.

And so, once upon a time, you tell yourself, passing this passing, once upon a time there was the kiss.

In Tautenberg.

The grassy fragrance. The gauzy air. The fertile afternoon.

Lou was walking in front of me up the path, her violet perfume drifting back. I was re-making a point. Humans, I was proposing, want to know the worst in a situation because eventually they tire of wanting to know the best. Everything totaled the yellowgreenness of the day.

And then Lou simply stopped ahead of me.

Time became a block of ice holding both of us motionless inside.

Lou simply stopped, simply turned, and, two short steps later, I was breathing her breath, her lips full open on mine.

I didn't know what to do with myself.

There were so many ideas not to entertain.

My body found itself leaning into her, and, leaning, I realized my eyes remained open. I wanted to see. There was so much to take in.

I could taste Lou's violet perfume on her softly plump tongue. Her hands ascended my back to cradle gently the base of my brain. My hands found themselves beginning to unbutton her blouse. They possessed maps of their own.

Our teeth ticked together. Once. She laughed quietly into my mouth.

My knuckles brushed the skin beneath her jaw.

More light.

More light, please.

She kissed me.

This, in any case, being the crux of the matter.

Lou kissed me on a path amid the gauzy yellowgreenness of the afternoon and, leaning, kissing, I studied her closed eyes moving beneath her moving lids, how seriously she took our stillness, after her breath filled my mouth with possibility.

Unless, I wonder, closed eyes moving beneath her moving lids, perhaps she was thinking something else?

Perhaps she was thinking, for example: *So this is what charity feels like.*

Or, merely: *What was that sound? And that one?*

I am not the person to say.

Johannes, a good student but hardly an exceptional one, doesn't strictly know.

It is one way or it is the other.

That is all that we can assert with any real confidence in the gap between sentences.

Assuming what I am experiencing is called *memory*, and not something else.

Not, say, the nature of a wish.

In every uncertainty, there exists a trace of revenge.

Look: Plato is blushing at what he has done to us.
At what he has not done.
And so the prince lies burning in his bed.

Outside his window the midnight moon hangs minus one black bite.

We are occupied.

We want to say that we are occupied.

We want to say it is

liver

Then you are watching a baritone busy dying on stage in one of Wagner's over-the-top bits in Bayreuth and your mind is wandering. You are trying to keep it in check but your mind is wandering and the whole interminable production has been about our invisible friend in heaven edenville alpha alpha nought nought one and there leans forward two rows down and three seats across from you a thirteen- or fourteen-year-old girl you cannot take your eyes off. Her hair reaches the small of her back in a long straight ponytail so blond it is white her eyes an outrageous blue her skin a translucence her dress black her rhinestone choker thoroughly unnerving. She leans forward rapt beside her parents elbows on knees attending her first opera and by her very presence negating it. You are trying to keep your mind in check but can't help thinking how it is almost impossible to forget the past except for a few moments at a time because you are part of everything you have ever seen read written but you must overcome yesterday swimming against history's current and then you are growing conscious of a muttering around you. You pull your eyes away from the girl look back at the stage and the baritone has departed the orchestra departed and in their place stands Hanswurst the Clown in a stark spotlight alone grinning palms on knees in a floppy blue sockhat red-and-yellow striped vest over pale blue shirt green pants seal-flipper shoes your face. He is wearing your mustache shaggy eyebrows white makeup a red dot on either cheek and you are on stage looking out at the audience in your seat listening to the muttering then the ambient perplexity then the amused curiosity then the faint frustration. Hanswurst raises a hand to his forehead Indian-style peers out knees bent scanning the horizon for signs of intelligent life. He stands upright lets his arms fall to his sides shoulders slack performs a brief softshoe stops grins his grin aging and disappearing. From nowhere he produces a colorful bouquet of balloons red blue yellow. He opens his mouth to speak thinks better of it closes his mouth opens his mouth again thinks better of it closes it again opens it. *O my brothers,* he says at last, *in conclusion, if you could see, thank you, it's been a pleasure, because up there, because in the sky, not to put too fine a point on it, because up there in the sky one can hear no B-flat, no A-sharp, no F, because up there in the sky you cannot see Germany, and so, in summary, in a word, to be brief, I hope I am making myself perfectly plain, so to speak, the willows fluttering along the banks of the pond, my childhood, my father at the foot of the stairs, these are what they refer to as the good old days, I can think of none better, because only when you have denied me will I return to you, if you could see, O my brothers, and so the dead live on, they are called music critics, the dead live on, they are called bankers, and so, to come to my pant, up there one can hear neither a G nor a D, neither major nor minor, because for the superfluous ones truth is a kind of forgetfulness, and so, in summa, Deutschland Deutschland über alles spells what, spells something, spells what, it's on the tip of my sister's tongue, non plus ultra, she förstering a new idea that will cull us all, this therefore amounting simply to another way of saying...of saying...whatever my point might in extenso prove to be, which is to suggest, thank you very much, which is to submit to your kindness that if you could see the future clearly you would hang yourselves after drowning your children, because Deutschland Deutschland über alles spells, yes, that's it, spells the end of German philosophy and the theater in which you're sitting is at present on fire. This building is alight. Get up. Get out. Abandon ship. You heard me. Vermin and children first. Save yourself. Save your diamonds. Save that beautiful, beautiful blond girl in the second row. Look at her boots. Look at her buckles. Look at that bolt of hair. I'm not joking. Rise. Do as I do. Because you have less than a minute. You have less than a moment. You are currently living at the lip of calamity. Smell the smoke. The heat at my back is unbearable. An instant more, and your chairs will explode into flames beneath you. Rise. Run. O my brothers, you're about to dance whether you like it or not.* A hush then coughs then the clinking of jewelry finding its way back to amused curiosity becoming low-key mirth becoming a single titter and then chuckles a rain of giggles like a communal understanding a general outbreak of hilarity laughter rolling back and forth across the crowd people rocking in their seats white molars catching light. The audience loves it this is the good stuff this is the gold. The blond girl is perhaps loving it most of all her laughter turning her features into a harsh gargoyle face down front. Hanswurst raises a hand to his forehead Indian-style peers out knees bent balloon bouquet buoying up behind him scanning the horizon for signs of intelligent life ten seconds nine eight then he hesitantly joins in on the merriment as the first seat blazes up and the one after that and the one after that and so on burning.

in some,
the heart grows old first

When he awoke several months after sampling Otto Binswanger's delicious cherries, Friedrich found himself in a spot that looked very familiar. He was more or less certain he was home in Naumburg unless (the idea continually tickled him) the spot where he found himself proved to be a replica of his home in Naumburg situated somewhere else entirely.

Still, wherever he was, every morning, weather permitting, his mother waited for him to dress in his best suit and accompanied him on a lovely walk through the lanes to the marketplace where they shopped, and every afternoon she wrapped him in a plaid blanket and tucked him into his special chair on the veranda where his mind felt instantly breezy. Sometimes he spent hours there taking great pleasure in the fields beyond the town wall. Sometimes he closed his eyes and let his breezy mind visit the minds of others. Occasionally he stared at the newspaper spread out in his lap when his mother was finished with it, counting to one hundred and folding the next sheet back to lend himself the appearance of reading, although in truth he found such an idea less and less attractive these days, given all the potential combinations of words.

This is what he was doing, mimicking the habits of reading, when he chanced upon the headline for an article about a new book by a man named Julius Klingbeil. He let his interest slide down into the meat of the text because Friedrich liked the sound *Klingbeil* made in his head. It reminded him of the jangle-clank of cowbells.

He concentrated very hard and crept forward and back across each sentence as if it were a town wall very much like the town wall surrounding Naumburg, and his job were to locate the small fissure in it through which he might see the streets and houses of its meaning. Klingbeil had been a colonist in the New Germania. From the start he worked tirelessly to make a go of it, but gradually became disaffected. Last year, convinced the wilderness had won, he returned home with his family to write a scathing account of his experiences there. He accused Förster of incompetence, deception, and tyranny. The other colonists, he said, had been deprived of their money. They were forced to purchase what they needed from Förster by a private system of exchange. They lived in severe barracks while Förster himself lived extravagantly in what amounted to a small estate stocked with European wine, an upright piano, and even a gramophone in the drawing room into which no one was invited.

Despite this, Klingbeil maintained, one couldn't be too terribly hard on the man.

After all, he lived under sway of his manipulative wife. It was no secret from the outset who really ran the show. Förster was Lisbeth's little tin soldier.

Sitting on the veranda that afternoon, reading, Friedrich felt a smile complete his features. It spread through his muscles like a sweet flu, and didn't leave him for a full week. Every morning, smiling, he accompanied his mother to the marketplace, followed her back to their house, and sat in the living room waiting for her to prepare his lunch. No sooner had they taken their special seats among the leafage after their meal together than Friedrich would respectfully inquire if she were finished with the morning paper.

Was it within the realm of speculation she might be done soon?

Might it be conceivable she was not too awfully far away from…?

Quickly tired of his badgering, Franziska would relent. Friedrich examined every page closely, holding it four centimeters from his nose, snuffling for further traces of Klingbeil.

It wasn't long before he located a second article.

The rightwing *Bayreuther Blätter* had condemned the ex-colonist's assault on the New Germania as libelous.

Lisbeth's letter-to-the-editor followed on its heels. In it, she explained Förster had suffered what she described as a *nervous attack*. False friends and the intrigues of enemies had broken her husband's spirit. She only hoped the wicked were satisfied.

Friedrich counted the number of words in her message: there were one hundred eleven of them.

He breathed in the ink.

It smelled like hours.

And then one muggy summer morning he came downstairs

to breakfast in his hospital gown, a yellow crust seeding his eye-lashes, took his place at the kitchen table, and looked up to find his sister sitting across from him.

He tried not to look surprised.

Her skin was the color of brown sugar. She seemed a little older, a little more existentially threadbare, than he recalled. She reached out and patted him on the wrist. Friedrich contemplated her chubby fingers. He wondered why she and Förster had never had children, and how she was able to carry Paraguay's awful climate with her all the way back to 18 Weingarten like this.

Have you seen my mother? he asked.

I'm here, Franziska answered from the stove where she was frying eggs and sausages, hot grease snapping.

Shall I perhaps be having cream cakes this morning?

Franziska exhaled noisily and set down her spatula.

This is what you have to say to your sister? *Shall I be having cream cakes?* You haven't seen her for a month of Sundays, she comes halfway around the globe to help me care for you, and this is what you have to say to her? Shame on you, Fritz.

It's too early for cream cakes, Lisbeth explained gently. Wouldn't you rather have some tasty eggs and sausages and toast instead?

I would prefer cream cakes, thank you. Several cream cakes. Let us say six.

Sit up straight, Franziska told him, arriving with plates. You're not having cream cakes, and you look like somebody's old creature, sitting hunched over like that.

Friedrich readjusted himself in his chair with regal exacti-tude and, taking stock, decided his best defense against these peo-ple would be the employment of logic.

I can eat any number of cream cakes, he began. Why do I have to eat eggs and sausages and toast when I can eat any number of cream cakes? I don't especially like eggs and sausages and toast. For example, orange marmalade tastes like rust. I don't see the argument of this breakfast at all…

He continued talking, although softer and softer, until his voice trailed off altogether and his lips remained in motion but nothing audible emerged between them.

Friedrich knew he had lost the skirmish. Neither his mother nor his sister was paying any attention to him. It was going to be eggs and sausages and toast or it was going to be air.

Flicking fluff off the left arm of his hospital gown, he tried to work out how his sister had journeyed from her letter to this table.

He could feel himself starting to perspire.

It felt like quicksilver worms in his armpits.

The only true music, he told himself, was the music of the swan song.

Besides, Franziska had taken her seat. She and Lisbeth were already embarked on a conversation of their own making. Friedrich didn't want to miss a syllable, because he had an inkling it might just prove to involve him. He heard many fascinating phrases in it that didn't upon first acquaintance seem to enjoy each other's company.

So he sat very straight, listened very closely, and, eyes shut tight, waited very courteously for his cream cakes to arrive.

When eventually he squints open his left to have a look around, hoping no one will notice, Friedrich finds himself, not in the kitchen over breakfast, but walking through a cold heavy downpour on his way home after school.

It is 1850. It is March. Last year his father died, and three months ago his little brother Joseph died, too.

Now his family is living in a different town and he is moving through a cold heavy downpour. All the other boys are running around him trying to get home, only Friedrich isn't running. Friedrich is walking with measured dignity along Priestergasse, holding his slate with his little handkerchief spread across it above his cap for protection. He is walking, jaw set against the heavy cold rain, just like a proper pastor should.

On another day in another place he would let the other boys have the weight of his tongue, but this afternoon he is new in the neighborhood, he doesn't know their names, and they wouldn't listen to him anyway because they are running because they are heathens.

Friedrich sees himself from above, as if he were standing in the second-story window of one of the houses lining the lane, moving through the words of psalm twenty-three, dangerous verbs and nouns falling away on either side of him like stones.

Priestergasse is the valley of the shadow of death and he has only three blocks to go and then he will be in domo Domini because every time you take a breath someone on the earthball dies only God has His reasons except He isn't telling what they are because we couldn't understand them even if He did.

With every step, Friedrich feels someone die in China in Berlin in Cairo in medio umbrae mortis in Africa in Brazil in Rome non timebo mala in New York in Madrid in Vienna.

You can't help breathing, but only for so long, and people can't help dying.

There goes another one.

Every person enters the world the same way but leaves it differently and enormous armies drive forward toward the brink and spill over like…

Like rain.

Like millions of droplets of rain into God's cupped hands Who has His reasons and up at the next corner Friedrich's mother appears under her big black umbrella and Friedrich's chest eases because things will be better from here on out.

His mother is waving at him like a constable.

Friedrich wonders as he veers toward her if other people see other colors when they look at that umbrella indigo purple orange yellow fuchsia but they call what they see black and so everyone sees a singular creation thinking it is the same creation everyone else sees except it isn't really except they will die thinking it is and when I say green you see goldenrod how strange.

Quickly, quickly, his mother is waving. Her real name is Franziska. His father's real name was The Pastor. She has come to collect Friedrich. In the dim rainy light, her shins below her black dress and black cape appear grayblue.

The wet air smells like wet cobblestones and wet wool and wet wool smells like peepee.

All the other boys are darting around him, a flock of finches, and his sinuses ache from the cold and his good shoes make squishy sounds beneath him and simply because everyone else is doing something doesn't mean you have to do it too.

Friedrich approaches his mother with deliberate steps, people dying everywhere, other children birding past him, and she is waving *quickly, quickly, over the edge, precious, over the edge,* and as he enters earshot she says:

What in the world do you think you're doing, young man, dawdling in the weather this way?

But Mama, says Friedrich, startled, six centimeters away from her and looking up into her dark face under her dark umbrella, rain smashing down around him.

I have a good mind to leave you find your own way home. Look at your shoes. And your *handkerchief.* God in heaven.

But Mama...

Since when does my little boy behave this way?

But Mama, Friedrich says kindly, proudly, because she doesn't understand, because she is too big, because her shins are grayblue, the school rules say boys are strictly forbidden to jump and run when they leave for the day. They must walk home quietly and with good manners. And sometimes we must all do things we don't like to do, Mama, mustn't we?

Yet the peculiarity of the situation is this:

The peculiarity of the situation is that Friedrich is simultaneously looking up at his mother's dark face under her dark umbrella on Priestergasse, waiting for his cream cakes to arrive in the kitchen at 18 Weingarten, and lying on his side somewhere in the infinite attic, head cradled in elbow crook, knees fetaled up to his swollen belly, trying to sleep and sweating profusely.

It is just like Prometheus, only without the hope of Heracles, and every morning a vulture midnight.

No matter what he does, they simply won't leave his liver alone.

Friedrich listens to air displace air in his nasal passages, a theory maturing inside him.

He isn't awake at all.

No.

It only seems that way.

He is in actuality dreaming within a larger dream within a larger dream, like a succession of Russian nesting dolls, and in one of these dreams his mother is saying to him from across the kitchen table, a piece of toast hovering before her lips:

Look at you. God in heaven. What have you done now?

Done, Mama?

His mouth is messy with eggy mush.

Your gown, Lisbeth adds, pointing with her fork. It's a fright, Fritz.

Friedrich consults his chest and discovers he isn't sweating at all. His hospital gown is soaked through with blood from neck hole to hemline. Blood steeps down his arms and legs. Trickles from the soggy cotton, dribbles off his chair, accumulates in a puddle on the floor beneath him. He contemplates the muck attentively, raises his head, and attempts an explanation:

It appears I must have nicked myself shaving.

Franziska chucks her toast onto her plate in disgust.

Lisbeth assumes the pained expression of someone who has just nipped the fleshy lining of her cheek.

Friedrich attempts to make himself very small, commencing covertly to pat himself down, feeling for the source of the leak. He can't seem to locate it. Or, rather, he can seem to locate it, and it is everywhere. He is hemorrhaging from every pore of his body.

Well, Lisbeth says at length, our family breakfasts certainly aren't what they used to be when Papa was alive, are they?

You see? says Franziska. You see? This is exactly what I've been trying to tell you. Only how can one commit such things to letters?

Lisbeth forks in another mouthful. Chews. Reflects.

I'm in the family way, Friedrich announces.

What? says Lisbeth.

I didn't mean for you to find out like this, but there you have it. Ex ovo: peccatum originale. I believe in our species that would make you the auntie and you the grannams. The Nietzsches propagate.

Lisbeth looks at Franziska.

Be a good boy, Fritz, will you, she says, turning back, and pass the butter. She reaches for her teacup and sips her Earl Grey. Goodness, she adds, such an unholy appetite for a widow...

Friedrich blinks, and when he opens his eyes again he sees Lisbeth sitting alone, not in the kitchen, but at her writing table in the pink parlor in the Archive directly below his room, one of his letters folded in its envelope before her.

She has waited until this evening's guests have gone. The Archive is finally quiet, Fritz finally asleep, and now she is sitting alone with her back to the art-nouveau stove that reminds her, with its rounded edges, fluted panels, and mass, more of a pipe organ than what it really is. From this spot, she will be able to hear her brother should he wake.

Fritz has been sleeping less and less lately despite the opium, rising into panicked roars in the middle of the night, disoriented, frightened, and her heart flies out to him.

It is August. It is Weimar. It is 1900. Lisbeth will edit this letter and perhaps another until she is too tired to concentrate, then retire to the guestroom. It is a relatively small, relatively austere space built for visiting scholars, but she has already grown used to it. To her, it feels welcoming. Snug. She likes the idea Fritz and she are together again after all this time. Family is funny that way: one never argues more fervently, dislikes more fiercely, complains more openly, than one does with members of one's own—and yet it is to them one almost always winds back, with them one almost always keeps company, at the end.

Alwine busies herself around her, removing smudged schnapps glasses, dusting what the guests have touched, then pauses in the doorway until Lisbeth acknowledges her and asks if Frau Förster-Nietzsche might not care for a glass of warm milk.

Frau Förster-Nietzsche thanks her and declines.

Lisbeth has brought down from the guestroom a pen and sheaf of blank paper, and has extracted a letter folded in its envelope from the wooden cabinet full of Fritz's manuscripts. She unfolds it, flattens it out on the table, begins to read. She rubs her forehead, gummy with the night's heat, and sighs at how from the outset Peter Gast made such a botch of Fritz's unpublished work.

He collected all the wrong selections for his anthology and wrote a horrid series of misleading prefaces. In the early days, he had the audacity to refer to himself as Nietzsche's First Disciple. He tagged after him at a distance like some sort of pet chimp with a notebook. Yet he has consistently misunderstood her brother's every intention. Try as he might, he has been unable to perceive the Fritz within Fritz, the one that always knew what he was about, and so Lisbeth has had to begin again from scratch.

She fired the Jew, convinced her mother to make her Fritz's legal guardian, moved her brother and the Archive from Naumburg to Weimar so he could find suitable companionship among the spirits of Goethe, Schiller, Bach, Liszt, and Cranach, and here she is, sometime past midnight in this muggy parlor, helping her brother into history.

It is hard work, but it is enough. Fritz's books are selling better than they ever sold when he was himself. Individuals with the necessary credentials and acumen have begun to grant that her brother is no longer merely a flesh-and-blood being. He is a cause. Within him resides the embodiment of faith for a Germany that will chew up and spit out all this aimless decadence one sees around one every day. Esteemed visitors have begun to appear regularly to pay their respects. Lisbeth is only too glad to lead them up to her brother's room for a viewing. Imagine: Rudolph Steiner.

It is hard work, but it is enough. Lisbeth seldom finds herself in bed before one, seldom up a minute past five. She doesn't see as much of Fritz as she might like. She has little time for herself. Nonetheless, her effort reminds her of those exciting early days in the New Germania with Bernhard, before everything went sixes and sevens, before he reached for that horrid vial, and it is enough.

Her remaining family sleeping peacefully above her.

The insubstantial scent her only brother has left on this letter before her.

The quiet and the comfort of this night in this room in this large house.

Lisbeth reads and rubs her gummy forehead and sighs and thinks of her mother's delicate hands, how bluewhite they looked just after she had turned her face to the wall in bed, drew them up beneath her chin, and died, and Lisbeth will never lose what she had with Fritz no matter what happens. She stops reading in midsentence. No, she decides. No. All this godless talk simply won't do. Fritz is wandering again. Her brother is losing his place, wafting among countrysides, at home nowhere. Fritz isn't saying what Fritz means to say, and it is up to Lisbeth to make sure he does. She owes that much to tomorrow. This, if nothing else, is what family is for—to look after one another, make everything come out right in the long run.

Lisbeth nods no and picks up her pen.

She releases a sheet of paper from the sheaf, and commences recopying Fritz's letter in a reasonable facsimile of his handwriting, crafting it into the thing that it wants to be deep down inside itself.

1 a.m.

My Dearest Deficiency—

In your head.
You write it in your head.
To help pass this funeral without end.

My Dearest Deficiency—
At the risk of seeming perhaps somewhat too forward, I should like to take this opportunity to draw your attention to the seemingly unavoidable fact that it has been nine full seconds since last I heard from you.
Nine or ten.

Let us say no more than a dozen.

This state of affairs provides me with occasion to speculate that, now and again, here and there, one's life persists well after one has, as the heifers have it, already joined the great majority.

In any case, I have wet myself again.

I am almost sure of it.

I tried to hold it, naturally, but some gestures reveal themselves to be more human than others.

These things happen.

To everyone.

Incessantly.

Which is merely another way of saying that my body has taken it upon itself to remind my llama just who really matters every minute of every day, and, so, please come collect me. Quickly. Polyphemus is at the window, waving his handkerchief.

Send our secret signal, whatever that secret signal may prove to be, and he will let down his hair for you, if he has hair, if he can let it down, because, at the end of the day, pissito ergo sum.

Call it one of the simple pleasures.

Speaking of such things, you should see the world as I do from up here on the cross. It looks much like Rome, only with bowties and jack-boots—making it difficult, although far from impossible, to embody every voice in history. Think, for example, of Wagner's dirty breath. The very soul of the elderly expelled from his mouth. It is in this manner that we greet the immortals. Which puts me in mind of the question that I have been meaning to ask you:

Do you happen to remember the name of that place?

You know the one I mean: the place you think of when I ask: Do you happen to remember the name of that place? The town of white cats. They followed Fredericus through the streets like a herd of beggar ghosts.

I am speaking of the village poised on the slatey green lake, mountains lifting sharply on all sides, proof positive that every philosophy is a category of involuntary memoir, every autobiography an act of autojustification.

Sils-Maria.

Yes: that's it.

It was extremely pleasant dining at the local restaurant there every evening, surrounded by people, so long as I didn't have to put myself through the trouble of speaking with any of them. They are best enjoyed at a distance. This is what others are good for: making space feel fuller. Otherwise, eventually, every one of them will prove a great disappointment. The limitless inadequacies. The myriad ways a person can let another person down.

People, I want to say, have much the same purpose, then, as pet dogs: to make the lonely feel less so, while preventing pre hoc any appearance of significant communication.

Dogs, that is, exist for those who wish to dominate another human being, but lack the will to do so, and are thereby obliged to purchase their love and power at the market in the form of a filthy, groveling beast with a propensity to chew one's rugs and nose one's privates.

Unlike, cela va san dire, cats.

Cats, let it be said here and now, know what they are about.

You may always share their superb hygienic existence, but you may never command it.

I recall how they used to follow me among the Italianate buildings, grillwork in windows, on my brisk daily stroll without you, then slowly fall away, leaving me to my own devices as I pushed forth onto the lakeshore path, walking stick in hand, toward a nice cup of green tea and small cream cake or two in that little café in Sulej several kilometers away, before returning along the same course to continue the reconstitution of the universe, every hour punctuated by the gong of church bells.

The freezing air, you may recall, was spined with pinesap. The stream gushed out front of the buttermilk cottage, in a small room on the second floor of which my brother the prince sat writing. Loneliness was his tapeworm.

The word for the lovely garland trim on the buildings was sgraffito.

Sgraffito.

This embodies for me the real pleasure of hotels. I was always nearly overwhelmed with delight at entering one. Every bed was both mine and not mine, novel yet familiar, and at every desk waited a new book to be written.

You can really let yourself go in such spaces, every hotel room reminding you that your world can be different.

Even so, the door remains a perpetual option, which is to say I seem to be writing you a farewell letter.

Because, you see, my greatest mistake in life, it now occurs to me, arms and legs invisibling in this stillness despite my best efforts to the contrary, has been to read myself into you, when the real point is there was never a me inside you to begin with.

You were someone else all along.

Yourself, presumably.

One can only forgive so much. And hence I don't believe I shall be writing you again. Some things need to stop when the debts are paid. Even if one thinks one knows what is going to happen, the instant of its happening remains unlivable. Be that as it may, everyone departs a eunuch. I have had Caiaphas put in chains. Death spays us all in the final days of the grand carnival.

That said, I'm afraid there's no way for God to avoid being Himself. Some things are ineluctable. And with such a position come certain responsibilities. I have, by way of illustration, given form to this caricature. You may be as critical of it as you wish, and I shall be quite grateful—without, however, promising to make any use of your comments.

Mind you, I shan't be any trouble. One can only die in the future tense, on balance, and then only so many times. That will always leave us the white sun on the white mountains.

Please feel free to make any use of this letter that does not make the people of Basel think less highly of me.

Not there.

Here.

Hurry.

Close your eyes, or you won't be able to see a thing.

> *Your Fond Goat,*
> *Dionysus*

Post Scriptum: Informal dress the rule.

eyes

When you open your eyes you discover yourself in an empty hospital ward propped among pillows another bed another hot night covers folded down to your waist oil lamp stammering on your bedside table and you have had an operation. Your chest burn-throbs. An extremely thin dressing covers an extensive wound there the dressing is sodden with blood. You search for a cord a bell a way to summon the nurse but there is only you bare walls no beds save your bed no sounds save those your body invents and the pain from the wound swims back and forth across the surface of your cortex. You call out pause call out again nothing this doesn't look good. Enough is enough you tell yourself eventually enough is enough so you prepare to swing your legs over the side of your bed strike out in search of help but the burnthrob blackens when you attempt tensing your muscles so you sit very still and make yourself go away for a while. You try another shout make yourself go away for a while and when you return you appreciate the fact you will have to wait this one out contemplating the bloody dressing again looking away looking back the curiosity won't leave you alone. Employing the greatest care you raise your right arm pincer a flap all right you think you can do this you really can lifting and peeling back peeling back a little more and then below the thin dressing your rib cage is exposed. Your rib cage is exposed and among the bloodslosh you can see your own heart beating. Your skin is gone and you can see your own heart beating among the bloodslosh and you go away for a while and when you return you detect the secondary movement a trembling a small wet trembling skinless snout tiny skinless paws something wanting out of you something wanting air. Employing even greater care you raise your left arm bring it to the aid of your right fold back the dressing reach inside your chest cavity your ribs separating easily breastbone fractured for the occasion and push around your smooth lungs lift your heart from its nest beneath it the thing wanting to get out squirming. You set your heart on your belly and probing squeeze the small slippery trembling thing in your hands lift it free a blind writhing embryonic puppy skin stripped away purplepink muscle yellowish frog-egg fat blue vessel-webs this is what it is like for a man to give birth tiny mouth opening closing straining for air this is what it is like and you are a father now. You are a father and the notion is plentiful with pride accomplishment panic expectation. This is a lying-in hospital that's where you are a lying-in hospital sans midwives sans nurses sans doctors. It is just you and your newborn because this is how it has always been because you birth alone cross from opening to opening alone. Slowly a question gets to its feet at the back of your brain and you lift your newborn higher with one hand part its hind legs with the other squint make out a purplepink organ comprised of two purplepink organs it's a girlboy a boygirl a goybirl and you beam with wellbeing. If your sister could only see you now if your mother your father because from this moment forward someone will be coming for dinner every night behind your forehead. You lower your newborn to your breast what is left of your breast pet its head nosing for your nipple the first pinchy suckling pinpricks arriving because you are a father and *there there precious* you say settling back into your pillow grinning closing your eyes *there there* the visions commencing.

on involuntary bliss

Language is a flirt, Friedrich announces to no one, surveying the women lined up for his pleasure along the mahogany bar with their silk robes flapped open and their floppy breasts exposed like double-fisted sacs of white sadness.

The hefty madam with the smeared lipstick has told him to take his time, make his choice, and now he is busy choosing.

It is Cologne. It is February. It is 1865.

Yesterday, Friedrich, barely twenty-one, arrived to sing in the six-hundred-strong choir at the festival here, and today the noisy friends he made told him they were taking him out for a late dinner, but took him instead to this timber-and-plaster house down by the river.

Language is a flirt and some things are never symbolic, Friedrich says aloud for his own benefit. Narration helps him arrange the convolution of things. How, for instance, this drawing room is a silent detonation of crimson-and-gold chinoiserie: the drapery, the wallpaper, the overstuffed furniture, the patterns on the rugs.

How the chalky bluegray cigar haze tiers itself geologically through the air.

How standing in this place is like standing inside a woman's dress-up purse: overdone, overcrowded, mystifying.

Friedrich's hands drift up to help explain to him what it is he is thinking, but no one notices because his noisy friends are busy laughing and drinking and smoking in their shirtsleeves. Two are banging out a raucous beer-hall duet on the rattly upright piano in the corner. The women at the mahogany bar are waiting indifferently for Friedrich to make his decision while they hold their loose breasts in their palms like fishmongers palming their produce, or examine their incision-red fingernails, or scratch the backs of their necks and stare at the floor.

Choosing, Friedrich inhales deeply.

Eau de toilette. Beer. The sour declarations of the body.

Every brushstroke of breath and color and sound, every centimeter of flesh, feels unforgettable.

Most of the women are too old for him, caked with too much powder, rouge, mascara, eye shadow. One is so enormous she seems to have been over-inflated with a bicycle pump, another so underfed her buttocks seem to have crumpled away like a pair of old apples. Gravity has roughed them all up, gapped their teeth, thickened their noses, lightly brownly blotched their hands and forearms. If they pinched the skin beneath their chins and let go, it would remain pinched.

They suggest a motley family of circus performers.

Friedrich cannot make up his mind.

Until, that is, he sees the thirteen- or fourteen-year-old girl with the long straight ponytail so blond it is white: she is lingering behind the others.

With that, he understands everything will succeed easily in this formulation because outside the sky is icy clear, the moon a dappled whiteblue platter. Everything will succeed easily, and the girl with the long straight ponytail is wearing a rhinestone choker, modestly gripping closed her crimson-and-gold robe. She is looking left with her outrageously blue eyes, as if trying to bring the wide river into focus through the wall.

The hefty madam with the smeared lipstick yawps playfully beside him:

The young man fancies Ingrid, eh? Good for him! Good for him! He knows value when he sees it! Ingrid, dear, come! Come! Your date is waiting!

Ingrid flinches. Ingrid collects herself.

Expressionless, Ingrid pushes off the bar.

Friedrich watches her lurch, catch herself, and, in that instant, he realizes she is lame. A liquid warmth oscillates through him. She limps by without so much as meeting his eyes, left leg unbending, and is through the curtain of raucous piano music, through the curtain across the doorway, thumping up the staircase, and Friedrich is following.

At the top extends another corridor, this one unadorned, down which she leads him, ponytail a pendulum across her back. She counts off five doors wordlessly, swings open the sixth, and steps to one side. Friedrich strides past her into a flickery almost-darkness.

Except then he is standing, not in the room in Cologne, but in the middle of a slightly raised platform serving as stage in the Archive's pink parlor, looking out from behind his sister's face.

The first thing he comes to understand about Lisbeth this time is how very old and very frail she feels. Her padless feet are pounding, the enlarged joints in her hands aching. The sloppy squid of her uterus throbs. Lisbeth, standing, wants to take a lie-down.

The second thing he comes to understand is how animated she feels despite these setbacks. The intuition wheels through her that her legs will fold up beneath her like a brooding goose if she is obliged to maintain this pose a single second longer, yet this is precisely the price to pay for such glorious occasions, and she isn't about to change a thing. Fold away, she resolves. Fold away.

Friedrich looks down.

He is wearing a loose-fitting black dress with a wide white furry neckline and high black pointy-toed boots. He looks up. The parlor is choked with press and dignitaries. His sister takes a deep breath and, lips parted somewhere between a smile and an *oh!*, reaches forward with theatrical effect to offer Friedrich's walking stick to a short stern little man with greasy hair and thumb-tip mustache whom Friedrich has never seen before.

The parlor arrests.

The short little stern man reaches forward solemnly to accept the gift.

A war of flashbulbs discharges.

It is, Friedrich comprehends incrementally, the middle of October. It is 1934. That is to say, it is his birthday. Today exists in his honor. He would have been ninety. Instead, he is dead. Outside, it is windy and sharp. Inside, the short stern little man closes his grip around Friedrich's walking stick. For a few long seconds, they are both holding it aloft for the cameras to record. Their eyes meet. In that briefest period imaginable, the short stern little man winks at Lisbeth, and then the instant is over.

It has been hard work, Lisbeth reflects, more than four decades of it, but it has been good work, and worthwhile work, and here she is, managing the conclusion of it. Lisbeth is passing the torch. That is exactly how to phrase it. She is passing the torch, and there has been, she understands as she inhabits these glorious ticks of the clock, so much life in life.

The furious sun falling through the foliage out front of the main lodge at the New Germania compound.

These fiery heartbeats.

It has been hard work, but it has been good work, and Lisbeth will always remember what a smart dresser and perfect gentleman Adolf Hitler has been this overcast afternoon. She worried and worried about it. Who wouldn't? She had no idea what to expect from the man who possessed the confidence to carry the title *Führer*, and the strength of will to withdraw from the ragged disarray called the League of Nations. Only what in the world would such a person be like in the flesh after so much living had rushed him? When they met in the clutter of media men at the front door just past lunch, he bowed from the waist like a prince before a princess. Lisbeth found the gesture magnificent. His suit, a wheat jacket with dark trousers, looked even crisper than it had in the newspaper photographs. His handshake was a friend's.

Hitler smelled good, too.

Perhaps he was wearing cologne, or perhaps it was the cream he used to slick back his hair.

Either way, this is what she will remember most: how his clean lime fragrance enveloped her like a visual disturbance as she greeted him and led him into the foyer, up the stairs to Friedrich's room, inhaling merrily, journalists and dignitaries in tow.

The room was kept just as it had been the morning her brother died: the dark curtains, the empty walls, the narrow bed, the skinny bedside table, the lonely chair. Hitler stood in the doorway with his hands clasped before him, head lowered, grave. Then he crossed to the bed and laid a palm on Friedrich's pillow. He held this attitude for an unusually long period while the photographers scrambled to document it.

There are those who believe we are looking at a harsh winter, he commented as the flashes popped. I, however, am of a different opinion.

Lisbeth parted her lips somewhere between a smile and an *oh!* and brought them together again. She tried to think of something to say. Her mind remained impeccably void. She tried to think of something to say again. A filament of seconds elapsed.

She remembered, trying to think of something to say, a painting of his called *The Mountain Chapel* she saw on a visit to the Berlin museum: an orange-red spire on an orange-red-roofed white chapel dead center; washed-out bluishgreen mountains slanting in the same direction as the whitishblue clouds; a timber-and-plaster barn falling in from the left. Its simplicity and sense of solitude moved her, making clear just how much the Vienna Academy had misunderstood him, much the way the whole of Europe had misunderstood Fritz.

In connection with nothing, Hitler raised his head and asked with great earnestness:

Was he a dog person, your brother? I've often wondered about this.

Lisbeth deliberated.

I believe...I believe, if the truth be told, he favored cats slightly, she said. Although it is well known he never kept an animal himself.

Hitler conferred with the ceiling.

I'm partial to dogs myself.

Ah. Yes. Well. Of course there's much to be said on the species' behalf.

The pretty blond head of one of Hitler's male aides poked through the photographers.

Forgive me, it said, but everyone is ready.

Good *Lord*, Hitler declared, rising. Where did the time go? Frau Förster-Nietzsche, what a great pleasure it has been to meet you. Permit me...

He offered her his arm.

And now Lisbeth feels her fingers around her brother's walking stick loosening, letting go.

She realizes this is it: the torch coasting away from her.

This is how events feel falling into history.

She stands at the threshold of the last act and, with great self-consciousness, drops her eyes, urging her body to perform a painful little curtsey.

Down the steep grassy hill from the Archive, beyond the crypt in the cemetery comforting the remains of Goethe and Schiller, on the far side of Weimar's market square, the park sprawls along the Ilm River in a series of rolling lawns, winding gravel trails, artificial romantic ruins, flourishing trees.

In a glade somewhere along its banks, canine noses commence poking through the foliage. At first only two or three. Next six. Ten.

Sniffing the spring breeze.

Dobermans begin bounding from the bushes and gathering in the open, issuing growls, making moist sounds with their moist mouths, and, the pack complete, they set forth toward the city center.

Somewhere in a succession of dreams, Friedrich hears them.

Then hears them less.

Then hears nothing at all.

It is the most complete absence of noise he has ever experienced, like what he imagines standing alone on an arctic sweep on an entirely still night holding your breath would sound like, only more hushed, and *the dreams sometimes become so ferocious,* he comes to appreciate, lying there in the aural nothingness, *you have to wake up just to find a moment's rest.*

Ingrid is kneeling inelegantly between his legs while he sits on the corner of the slender bed, hands helping explain to him what it is he is thinking.

He is thinking there is only one candle in this room and it is flickering on the bedside table like a disturbed bat.

He is thinking thinking sometimes can be the opposite of useful.

He is thinking about how once, when he was twelve, Lisbeth burst into his room in the middle of the night and awoke him screaming *Fuck you! I hate you! I hate you! I hate you! I hate you!* and then slammed the door and returned to her own room, and how neither of them ever mentioned the episode again.

Friedrich, barely twenty-one, wears his choir suit from the waist up and from the waist down nothing but black socks and black shoes. They could use some polish. Listening to himself express his opinion on the matter, he observes his right hand desert the right side of his face to traverse the distance separating him from her, and come to rest atop Ingrid's head. Her scalp is oily, damply warm. The inside of Friedrich's mouth is vinegarish and sticky. He hears himself speaking, and wonders what he could possibly have to say at a time such as this.

Christians consign to hell everything that stands in their way, is what he could possibly have to say, *and pretend you are dead.*

His voice is gentle, a benediction.

Through the door, down the corridor, down the staircase, his new friends are banging away at the rattly upright. In the next room, a woman is moaning and giggling and moaning and giggling. Blanketed over her sounds are masculine ones so low, so deep, that Friedrich can feel more than hear them.

There are no paintings on the whitewashed walls. There are no rugs on the plank floor. Ingrid's robe has fallen open twice, and, twice, Friedrich has asked her to pull it closed, please.

Mouth full, she looks up at him.

From this angle, in this restless light, Friedrich can make out the shotgun pox-scars spattered across her cheeks.

In her very blue irises, he can make out perplexity.

Tonight your name is not your name, he announces gently, *and pretend you are dead.*

And suddenly the bed is gone from beneath him.

The ceiling from above him.

Friedrich is rising through hot air.

His thoughts hurrying past like sharks behind his eyes.

He feels less than numb   blank yes *blank* is a better word for what
he feels and there they are   there they are coming at him again

the dogs the pack of dogs

moving up the serpentine avenue

low-growling claws clittering across cobblestones

corpse of some small unidentifiable animal in their wake

no one noticing is the point no one paying any attention because

because

catch your breath   that's it   give it a second   give it a second

the cityscape suspended in morning mist

Weimar under siege

everyone sleeping and Weimar under siege

The problem with patients, plump Doctor Hildebrandt tells himself somewhere else, rereading his notes, left buttock elevated for support on the corner of the large desk against which he leans, is they have the custom of conceiving themselves as individuals.

Originals, they might say.

Take, for instance, the young man currently waiting on the other side of the door in the outer office. He announced with a certain degree of self-importance that he was a student of philology at the university, while making several nebulous references to an aristocratic ancestry designed to impress the physician into doing smart work. Yet the poor wretch looked anything save aristocratic. He looked, in point of fact, miserable: undernourished, skin dry-cheesy, weak eyes sunken and bruised behind his spectacles. He complained of a perpetually sore throat, sore joints, and headaches so ferocious he referred to them as *godsplitters*.

Godsplitters.

Doctor Hildebrandt liked that so much he wrote it down.

He shifts from his large left buttock to his large right buttock and his desk criticizes his decision.

It is Leipzig. It is September. It is 1867. The problem with patients, plump Doctor Hildebrandt is telling himself, is how they fail to understand they are neither more nor less than the sum of various afflictions conversing through the species across time. Take our young man here. The doctor had a fairly good idea about his diagnosis even before asking the fellow to please remove his shoes and socks so he could inspect the bottoms of his feet. The student of philology looked at him as if he, the student, were somehow above such exhibitions. But there they were, naturally: the reddish-brown spotty rashes across his soles. His lymph glands were inflamed as well.

The message was unmistakable: bad blood was having a word with him. Doctor Hildebrandt came across such cases every week or two. Everywhere you looked, you heard bad blood speaking.

It was nature's way of bringing the fagged-out lines of the well-to-do to a diffident close.

Pushing off his desk with a cumbersome shove, he clears his throat in order to clear his head. Lowers his clipboard. Runs a hand through his stonegray hair and straightens his bowtie.

When the message is bad blood, it is best to remain mum on the matter. If there is nothing to be done, then there is nothing to be done. This young man has a good twenty years ahead of him before things begin turning nasty, another ten beyond that before the biological message will have been wholly delivered. Why trouble him with forecasts today? It would be tantamount to walking up to a perfect stranger in the street, tapping him on the shoulder, and announcing: *Excuse me, sir, but someday you're going to die. I don't know when, obviously, but you are. I just thought you might like to know.*

Information like that isn't news. Information like that is tautology.

Plump Doctor Hildebrandt ambles across the room and swings open the door leading to his outer office, an artificial smile blasted across his countenance.

Voice full of pep, he proclaims to the poor wretch standing before him:

Herr Neski, you must be an excellent student. Do you know how I can tell this?

Nietzsche, Herr Doktor. The name is Nietzsche.

I can tell this because you have clearly exhausted yourself with your studies. And do you know what time it is now? It is time to take my advice. Listen to your new physician. Slow down. Just for a week or two, of course. Just for a week or two. Nothing precipitous. Long enough for your strength to return. That's all. Sleep in. Enjoy the fine food our fair city has to offer. Eat rich meat. Drink red wine. Indulge yourself. You will feel like a new man before you know it.

Surprised, longing to be encouraged, Friedrich pushes his oval wire-rimmed glasses up on his nose.

You're saying there's nothing wrong with me?

I'm saying there's nothing a little rest and relaxation won't help immeasurably, Herr Nitzki. Do me a favor, would you? Smoke a fine cigar in my honor tonight. Take a glass of brandy before bed. Will you do that for me?

I'm not sick, then? I feel like I feel, but you're telling me I'm not sick?

Plump Doctor Hildebrandt blocks the doorway separating his outer from his inner office with his buoyant, considerable presence.

And beams.

Thinking about trying not to think, Friedrich carefully arranges Ingrid's limp body facedown on the slender crisply made bed.

He folds up her robe across her back and spreads her legs, vigilant not to bend the bad one. Drapes her ponytail over her head like a blond exclamation point. In the top half of his choir suit and his black socks and his black shoes, Friedrich sits rigidly on the corner of the mattress and enjoys how her skin blotches and unblotches in the dim anxious light.

It is this easy to remove himself from life. Two days ago he was a student. Three hours ago he was a singer. Now he is this, here, far away from everything.

He is this, here, counting the number of paintings on the wall and the number of rugs on the floor, arriving at the sum of nil. He rises, crosses to the window, and parts the frayed curtains that don't close all the way. Touches the pane with his fingertips. It occurs to him: *I am leaving traces*. There, below, is the empty nightblue moonlit street and, opposite, a row of two-story buildings whose colors Friedrich cannot determine in this odd, stark, silvery light.

He draws the curtains as far as they will go and, feeling as if he has just entered a dream, returns to bed. Ingrid has not stirred. She remains so motionless the chance presents itself she may have ceased breathing altogether.

This room gives off an unpleasant odor of wood smoke, tar, musty linen, soap.

Thinking and not thinking, Friedrich observes his left hand desert the left side of his face to traverse the distance separating him from her and come to rest between her smooth white girlish thighs. Her neck and shoulders so relaxed. He inserts a thumb into her. She is wet inside. He hears himself speaking like a parent to an upset child.

In Germany we have always been an accident, he is saying, *and you are lying on your stomach because if you give people as much freedom as they want their first instinct will be to imitate each other and don't show me your face.*

With his other hand, he takes Ingrid's left wrist tenderly and brings it up onto her back onto her folded-up robe below her shoulder blades.

He has entered the kind of dream where you know you are dreaming, and you can change anything you want however you want.

No one is watching. It is this easy.

They dress the same and hope the same and ask so much but give so little, he is saying. *This is the eventual hymn to each and every friendship.*

He takes Ingrid's right wrist and brings it up onto her back, onto her folded-up robe below her shoulder blades, and crosses it over her left wrist. Her arms form a W. He holds her wrists that way with one hand. Ingrid remains unmoving.

Friedrich reviews his work.

He takes her right wrist and lowers it, brings it up and around, rests it on the back of her head so her fingers crook slightly off into space.

He extracts his left thumb from between her legs, reaches forward, searches for her mouth, and inserts it between her lips. She is wet inside. Her incisors jaggy. Her tongue is a strip of warm liver. Everything is slack.

Because you are lying on your stomach because in Germany we are both mistakes because Paul was always the greatest apostle of vengeance, he is saying. *The believer never belongs to himself. I have told you this before and will tell you this again and I have made me listen to myself. Now you are lying on your stomach. The believer never belongs to himself and so he must always be used up by others. This is what we refer to as devotion. Sometimes it is painful and sometimes it is like entering a dream like the dream we have entered tonight. We must be used up by it and don't show me your face.*

Friedrich extracts his thumb from her mouth and traces it across her cheek, along her neck, down the knuckle-sized knobs comprising her vertebrae. He slips it into the crevice between her firm girlish buttocks, probing, and, with steady insistent pressure, pushes into her, and she is slimy inside. Beyond her sphincter opens a hot looseness and no one is watching.

He counts to thirty. Counts to thirty again. Lifts himself onto his knees.

Lovingly, he separates her legs farther, careful not to bend the bad one, and, speaking all the while, descends little by little into Ingrid's abrupt wakefulness.

Somewhere else, rising through the darkness, Friedrich understands his heart may have stopped, and posits that one's final hours might last forever. It feels as if what he has always thought of as inside is in the process of becoming what he has always thought of as outside.

The body growing increasingly   what   *profuse*

profuse being the word for what the body is increasingly becoming

fluids general

call it a leakage

a selfseepage into the   right

well put

your inner being expressing itself with conviction

shit and stupidity

stupidity and shit

what good I wonder is a mouth for thinking

if these are the thoughts it

what do you think

you think that after forty years one's face becomes an achievement
after fifty a warning   and in the prince's final hours a simple
superfluity because   because

is this it then are we finally leaving

her full lips full and

Silk robe tugged and tucked back into place, Ingrid sits primly on the edge of the bed.

She stares at the floorboards, reflexively wiping her mouth with the back of her hand, while Friedrich, spiked in place, finishes buttoning his fly.

He can't stop staring at her, can't stop reliving in his mind's eye the events that unraveled between them. He can't stop believing how plentiful the universe is, how thrillingly hectic with potential.

Done with his trousers, he steps forward and rests a palm on Ingrid's scalp. She continues staring at the floorboards. Drops her right hand to her lap, where her left already rests. Braces for whatever might come next. Friedrich bends from the waist, fingercombs her hair out of the way, whispers into her ear kindheartedly:

A philosopher is someone who can turn on his amnesia at will. This is what we call compassion. We must always leave in due course and thank you for your gift.

He delivers a peck upon her oily damp forehead.

Straightening, he pats down the front of his choir suit.

He turns, strides to the door, and, chin held almost undetectably too high, steps into the corridor, where it strikes him with alarm that he can no longer catch his breath.

Because he sees Lou riding away on horseback across a meadow, lush green landscape suspended in leaden mist.

His perspective is that of a low-gliding hot-air balloon.

No matter how hard he tries, he cannot manage to catch up with her, slip behind her face for a few flashes, before she is rushing away again, her shadowy form vanishing into vapors, dropping back into the open, vanishing, dropping back.

It is the Rhine Valley. It is 1912. Last year Lou made Sigmund Freud's acquaintance at a soirée in Vienna. Now she is arranging

an article in her head for his journal, *Imago*, and she is trying to remember something. The fog will clear soon and she will remember
it and it is April.

Yes: she is trying to remember if Friedrich ever actually
kissed her.

She is trying, but it was a very long time ago. They were
standing on a path in the woods, yes, or was that Rilke, no, it was
Friedrich. She remembers that terrible sister of his. He called her
his *llama*.

Lou is trying, but she cannot bring the incident in question to
mind with anything like clarity.

She loved him, needless to say. She loved him, but never like
that. She loved him like you might love a wonderful teacher who
changed your life utterly when you were young, but then you grew
up and grew away and you don't even think about him very often
anymore. That is how she loved him.

Did he actually kiss her, or almost actually kiss her, or only
look as if he wished he might actually kiss her, but knew she would
never go along with such a silly wish?

Surely the memory is inside her.

The memory is inside her, and all she has to do is concentrate
to locate it. Dour Sigmund tells her this all the time. The examined
life, he says, is a life about discipline. The examined life is a life
about the strength of intellect to convert phenomenon into x-ray.

Except the truth is Lou can't find the memory inside her no
matter how hard she searches and so

and so

and so she shakes off the remote irritation, turns her knees in, and encourages her horse from trot to canter.

Friedrich is falling behind.

The last thought of hers he experiences revolves around the prospects for breakfast that lie before her. Lou will return to the cottage where she and her husband are holidaying. She will join him at the table in the garden and tell him about her ride, the progress she is making on her article. He will listen as if interested. Lou will opt, she believes, for nothing more involved than cheese and bread and a glass of white wine, no, champagne, no, white wine, and she will spend the rest of the morning writing down her thoughts. This afternoon is too far away to contemplate.

And now she is putting more and more distance between them.

She is moving very fast.

Friedrich tries to catch up, except her spectral form becomes the size of a swan becomes the size of a swift and Lou is plunging into a graywhite bank and she is there and she is less there and then she is nowhere at all.

And that's the worst, Friedrich thinks, rising through hot darkness: when all the voices fall silent

                              when you strain to hear them

                              and hear nothing instead

you straining and   there was love for you once   how the air
was moving   the body assuming any position it likes now   except the one that can sustain it

not a single hand laid upon us

                                                    that's the worst

you somehow always expected more

how she turned on the path

we are I want to say time's way of contemplating things

                                              how she turned toward you

in the gauzy yellowgreen sunshine

your mouth loose against the

today apparently can't do much more to us

catch your   no   how it feels   how the clouds move

another few thoughts

good   that's good   a little farther

how the day shifts above you   yes   how you stood there

looking up

a swarm of red blue yellow balloons

drifting   they are drifting

everywhere the wild scrape of claws on pavement

tongues lapping air

barks splitting the season

heavy bodies thudding heavy bodies in the dash over walls

through the hedges

                                        from the shadowcrowded alleys

                    across bridges

through beautiful linden tunnels

dobermans throwing themselves into the lanes of my head

yes   good   yes   now we're finally getting somewh

fourth part:
the world is transfigured
& all the heavens are full of joy

noon

Franziska sprawls indecorously in her unmade bed, propped among a snowbank of pillows, knees raised, legs spread, straining against the pain sluicing through her in stunning swells.

On her face, splodged pink and slicked with sweat, a look that says *get away from me.*

Her matted hair dangles around her shoulders in sharp-tipped strings. Her lacy mint maternity gown has been hiked to her armpits. Her hands are red lungs breathing atop her tummy.

It is Röcken. It is 1844. It is mid-October and the weak autumn sun is presumably hanging behind a high haze like a diaphanous lemon drop outside the window; only the curtains are drawn, the bedroom dim and close.

Franziska sprawls indecorously, huffing, trying to lose herself. Her midwife, a severe woman whose barrel chest sits oddly atop her petite hips and stunted legs, takes another step in her direction with a damp cloth and reaches out. The shocking pain has made Franziska forget the woman's name, yet she still has the strength to roll her eyes toward her with a look that says *get away from me; if this is how life comes to pass, don't talk; if this is part of what God didn't say, then leave me alone.*

And the midwife does.

She retreats to a chair by the curtained window and sits at attention, her toes unable to touch the floor.

The first spasm struck late last night. Franziska was sewing in her rocking chair across the sitting room from her husband, who was reading on the sofa, and then she was crying out in disbelief.

Eighteen, she has been married almost twelve months and this is humiliating. It hurts like a carving knife hurts. Her body is issuing horrible metallic odors. Franziska is not frightened so much as outraged by what is happening to her. She is trying to lose herself, trying to be on the other side of the curtains in the garden under that weak autumn sun—kneeling, perhaps, among the remains of her flowers, wandering among the furry willows shedding around the fishponds.

She knows she has to do this thing. She knows she has to do it by herself. This is how women become stronger. Women become stronger by living in another place that is this dimension and that is not this dimension. And, next, Franziska is no longer here. Instead, she is winding through the streets of the village beside The Pastor on their way to church one summer Sunday blue and bright as a chip of lapis lazuli. Their relationship, she takes in as they stroll, dipping their chins in unison as they pass members of the congregation along the lanes, is that they touch by not touching.

Content enough with this state of affairs, she gives into movement, tilting her face up slightly toward the agreeable heat. Franziska feels good. She feels in step with the village around her and the fields around the village.

She suspects that she is becoming the sunlight itself until something mulekicks her in the abdomen, and she screams again, and the sluicing pain turns the bedroom into saffron light.

Later, after her body allows her to think, after time commences passing once more, Franziska is a mother.

She opens her eyes without lifting her head from the pillow, and The Pastor is standing at the foot of her bed. His shoulders are loose with relief and pleasure, his skin a little grayer than it had been the night before, his hair a ruffled animal. He hasn't slept, and, through her grogginess, Franziska loves him for it.

He is busy speaking, saying a modest little prayer, voice flushed with pride, and as the severe midwife dabs Franziska's forehead with the damp cloth, Franziska notices that while she was gone someone tugged down her maternity gown into place, tugged up the covers, and opened the curtains. Appropriate again, she becomes aware of something warm and active in her arms.

She concentrates on moving her head. The muscles in her neck and back are numb. She focuses and, in gradations, succeeds in adjusting her weight.

With great effort she looks down, and she is a mother.

Franziska's baby boy emerged without a sound, the midwife explains in low reverent tones as she dabs Franziska's forehead with the damp cloth. She has never seen anything like it. He emerged without a sound, and his silverblue eyes are alertly taking in the planet.

Look at him, the midwife says. He has been having his own ideas for months. You can tell these things.

Outside a cart clatters by. Someone yells a chipper greeting to the driver. The driver yells a chipper greeting in return. The baby boy's silverblue eyes follow the noise with quiet blind interest.

At the foot of the bed, The Pastor concludes his prayer by announcing forty-nine years ago today the reigning Prussian king, Friedrich Wilhelm IV, was born, and he is a good leader, a good man, and a good Protestant. Their son will take on his name. Watching her baby boy watch the world for the first time, Franziska has no opinion about this. Eighteen years ago, just a few miles from this spot, her mother held her like she is holding her own child. It strikes her that cradled in her arms she is carrying generations.

A stillness dilates through the room. Everyone, Franziska understands with satisfaction, is watching her son watching. Friedrich is making small soundless sucking movements with his lips.

Look at little Fritz, says the midwife. He is kissing the future.

Again.